Praise for Lynn Austin

"A rich and enchanting historical reading experience."

"Austin transports readers into the lives of her characters . . . giving them a unique take on the traditional World War II tale. Readers won't be able to turn the pages fast enough."

"In Lynn Austin's tantalizing domestic drama *If I Were You*, desperation and forgiveness are part of a classic upstairs/downstairs plot."

"Lynn Austin is a master at exploring the depths of human relationships."

"*If I Were You* is a page-turning, nail-biting, heart-stopping gem of a story. . . . [I] sighed with satisfaction when I reached the final page. *So* good."

"*If I Were You* is sure to garner accolades and appeal to fans of novels like *The Alice Network* and *The Nightingale*."

JULIE KLASSEN, author of *A Castaway in Cornwall*

"With her signature attention to detail and unvarnished portrayal of the human heart, Lynn Austin weaves a tale of redemption [in *If I Were You*] that bears witness to Christ's power to make all things new."

SHARON GARLOUGH BROWN, author of the Sensible Shoes series and *Shades of Light*

"*If I Were You* is . . . a compelling read, beautifully written, celebrating the strength of faith and the power of sisterhood."

CATHY GOHLKE, Christy Award–winning author of *Night Bird Calling*

"*If I Were You* is a beautiful story about courage, relentless love, and the transforming power of forgiveness."

MELANIE DOBSON, award-winning author of *The Curator's Daughter*

THE WISH BOOK CHRISTMAS

Also by Lynn Austin

The Wish Book Christmas

LYNN AUSTIN

Tyndale House Publishers
Carol Stream, Illinois

Visit Tyndale online at tyndale.com.

Visit Lynn Austin's website at lynnaustin.org.

Tyndale and Tyndale's quill logo are registered trademarks of Tyndale House Ministries.

The Wish Book Christmas

Designed by Lindsey Bergsma and Libby Dykstra

Edited by Kathryn S. Olson

Published in association with the literary agency of Natasha Kern Literary Agency, Inc., P.O. Box 1069, White Salmon, WA 98672.

Unless otherwise indicated, all Scripture quotations are taken from the *Holy Bible*, King James Version.

Isaiah 9:6 in the epigraph is taken from the Holy Bible, *New International Version,® NIV.®* Copyright © 1973, 1978, 1984, 2011 by Biblica, Inc.® Used by permission. All rights reserved worldwide.

The Wish Book Christmas is a work of fiction. Where real people, events, establishments, organizations, or locales appear, they are used fictitiously. All other elements of the novel are drawn from the author's imagination.

For information about special discounts for bulk purchases, please contact Tyndale House Publishers at csresponse@tyndale.com, or call 1-855-277-9400.

Library of Congress Cataloging-in-Publication Data
Names: Austin, Lynn N., author.
Title: The wish book Christmas / Lynn Austin.
Description: Carol Stream, Illinois : Tyndale House Publishers, [2021]
Identifiers: LCCN 2021006530 (print) | LCCN 2021006531 (ebook) | ISBN 9781496452528 (hardcover) | ISBN 9781496452535 (kindle edition) | ISBN 9781496452542 (epub) | ISBN 9781496452559 (epub)
Subjects: LCSH: Christmas stories. | GSAFD: Christian fiction.
Classification: LCC PS3551.U839 W57 2021 (print) | LCC PS3551.U839 (ebook) | DDC 813/.54--dc23
LC record available at https://lccn.loc.gov/2021006530
LC ebook record available at https://lccn.loc.gov/2021006531

Printed in the United States of America

27	26	25	24	23	22	21
7	6	5	4	3	2	1

For Lyla and Ayla

For to us a child is born, to us a son is given . . .

Prologue

DECEMBER 1951

Bobby Barrett stepped off the kindergarten school bus and his foot sank into a pile of fresh snow. Some of the snow fell inside his galoshes and soaked into his socks, making him shiver. He couldn't remember there being this much snow back home in England, where he was born.

"Yay! It's snowing again!" his friend Harry Dawson cheered as the bus roared away. "If you stick out your tongue, you can catch snowflakes on it, like this."

Bobby watched, then imitated Harry, opening his

mouth wide and sticking out his tongue. Bobby had moved to America only a year and a half ago with his mum, but Harry had lived here ever since he was a baby. He was always teaching Bobby new things. Snowflakes fell from the gray sky like feathers from a torn pillow, and they tickled Bobby's tongue as they landed on it.

"Come on, let's make footprints," Harry said a moment later. They stomped through the snow that had piled up on their neighbors' lawns as they made their way down the block to the house they shared. Mummy had been friends with Harry's mum for a long, long time, and now they all lived together in the same little house.

"I love it when it snows," Harry said. "Know why?"

"Why?"

"Because that means Christmas is coming, and Christmas means toys! Lots and lots and lots of toys!"

"Where do the toys come from?" Bobby asked.

"From Santa Claus, silly! You tell him what new toys you want and he brings them to your house on Christmas. Didn't Santa Claus ever come where you used to live?"

"You mean Wellingford Hall? In England?"

"Yeah."

"Hmm. I remember Father Christmas," Bobby said, "but I don't think I remember lots of toys."

Harry dropped to his knees and scooped up a pile of snow between his mittens, packing it together to make a ball. Bobby dropped down to do the same thing and felt the cold snow soaking through his mittens and the knees of his corduroy pants. He hoped Mummy wouldn't get mad at him for getting all wet.

"Santa Claus is very rich, and he likes giving toys to children," Harry said. "He left some under the tree for us last Christmas and some more at Nana and Granddad's house, remember?"

"I don't know. Maybe." Everything had been new and strange last year after he and Mummy had sailed across the ocean on a big boat. America was loud and noisy and hard to get used to compared to the peace and quiet of Wellingford Hall. Everyone was always in a big hurry here, and they talked funny. It had taken a while before Bobby could understand what people were saying. Bobby had wanted to leave America at first and go back home, but Mummy said they couldn't.

Harry stretched his arm back and threw the ball of snow as far as he could. Bobby did the same, but his ball fell apart, and the loose snow fluttered to the ground. Harry was better than Bobby at everything.

"Come on, let's run," Harry said. "I'm hungry! I hope your mommy made hot dogs for lunch."

Dogs? For lunch? An old woman was walking toward them with a big yellow dog on a leash, and it took Bobby a moment to remember that the Americans called sausages "hot dogs." They weren't really made from dogs, Mummy told him. He backed away as the dog got closer, his heart beating fast. He was afraid of most dogs, and this one was very big and frisky. It tugged on the leash as if it wanted to get away, and the lady had to pull back hard to make it stop.

"Hi, doggy," Harry said, waving. The dog looked at Harry and barked really loud, making Bobby's heart race even faster. He turned and ran the rest of the way home without waiting for his friend, hoping the dog wouldn't chase after him and eat him.

He arrived home breathless, beating Harry through the door for once. Mummy had lunch waiting for them on the kitchen table—tomato soup with saltine crackers and bologna sandwiches. He took off his galoshes, coat, and mittens and slid onto his chair, beating Harry a second time.

"How was kindergarten today?" Mummy asked as Bobby bit into his bologna sandwich.

Harry answered before he had a chance to. "We had fun! We painted pictures using our fingers. The paint felt all squishy and cold."

"I didn't like it," Bobby said. He had worried that the paint wouldn't wash off afterwards and he would have colored fingers forever. "Why don't they let us use paintbrushes in America?" he asked.

Harry shrugged his shoulders. "Because then they wouldn't be called finger paints, silly."

Bobby remembered what else they'd done in school today and hurried to tell his mum before Harry did. "Mummy, guess what? We're going to be in a play at school, and you and Harry's mum and Nana and Granddad can all come and see us."

"A play? How nice. Do you know what the play is about?"

"It has a baby and a lot of sheep in it," Harry said. He was talking with his mouth full, which Mummy said not to do. "Most of the kids are sheep but me and Bobby and another boy are going to be three smart, rich men."

"No, the teacher said we're rich *kings*!" Bobby said.

"Like the king we have back home in England. We're going to wear crowns and everything!"

"That sounds lovely," Mum said. "I can't wait to see it." She brushed Bobby's hair off his forehead. Her hand smelled like flowers.

Harry finished his lunch first, leaving the crusts of his bread behind. Bobby copied him—he hated the dry crusts, too—then followed him into the living room, after putting his dishes in the sink. They were trying to decide what to play when Harry spotted a colorful magazine on the coffee table that hadn't been there when they'd left for kindergarten that morning. "Look, Bobby! That's Santa Claus—see? He's the one who's going to bring us toys for Christmas. Now do you remember?"

Bobby picked up the magazine and studied it. The cover showed a fat, white-bearded man in a red suit putting presents beneath a Christmas tree. Santa held one finger to his lips as if saying, *"Shh . . . these presents are a secret . . ."*

"He looks sort of like Father Christmas," Bobby said, "with his white beard. But Father Christmas wears a green coat, I think. And he isn't this fat." He opened the book to see what was inside and saw pictures of all sorts of toys.

Harry grabbed the book from him. "Oh, boy! Look at all these cars and trucks!"

"Mummy, is Father Christmas the same as Santa Claus?" Bobby asked as she walked through the living room. She was carrying a basket of dirty laundry on her way to the basement.

"Yes, love. Children call him by different names in different countries. By the way, did you and Harry forget that we're going to see Santa Claus in the Christmas parade tonight?"

"Tonight?" Bobby asked.

"Yes, after we eat supper."

"Yay!" Harry cheered, bouncing in place. "We can sit on his lap afterwards and tell him all the toys we want him to bring us."

Bobby couldn't imagine sitting on this plump, red-suited stranger's lap. He felt shy around people he didn't know. "I don't know what toys to tell him."

Harry waved the magazine. "Well, there's lots of them in this . . . this . . . What's this book called?" he asked Bobby's mum.

She bent over to look at the cover. "The Sears Christmas Wish Book."

As she walked away, Harry leaned close to Bobby

to whisper in his ear, "We'd better hurry if we're going to pick out all the toys we want to tell Santa about tonight. Come on." He sank to the floor, lying on his tummy, and opened the book to the toy section. Bobby stretched out beside him, excited at the thought of picking out a whole bunch of new toys. It wasn't even his birthday!

"Oooh! Look at these fire engines!" Harry said. "And Santa will bring us everything we want!"

"Everything?"

"Yes. But only if we're good. Bad kids get sticks and coal for Christmas."

"What's coal?"

"Black lumpy stuff that looks like rocks."

"What do the bad kids do with it?"

"I don't know. I guess they have to play with it because they don't have any toys. Listen, Bobby. We have to be real good from now until Christmas, okay?"

"Okay. How long is it until Christmas?"

"I don't know. Maybe your mommy does." They studied a few more pages of toys until Bobby heard his mum come upstairs from the basement again.

"Mummy? How many days is it until Christmas?" he called.

"Ehm . . . let's see . . . twenty days."

"Oh no!" Harry groaned, slapping his forehead.

"Is twenty days a lot?" Bobby asked him.

"Yes! That's like . . . all of your fingers and all of mine! We'll have to be good for a long time if we want lots and lots of toys."

Bobby sighed. This all seemed like a lot of work. But the toys pictured in this wonderful Wish Book dazzled him, and like Harry, he wanted all of them. Most of the toys in their bedroom and at Nana's house had belonged to Harry before Bobby moved in, and although Harry was pretty good about sharing them, Bobby wanted some new toys of his own. "Start at the beginning again and go real slow," he begged. "I need to remember everything."

"Okay, okay," Harry said, turning back to the first page of toys. "I want these Tinkertoys, don't you? We can build fun towers and stuff with them, see?"

"Yeah! I want them, too." They continued through the pages, turning them slowly, studying the pictures. By the time they reached the end, Bobby could hardly wait to see this red-suited Santa Claus tonight and tell him about all the wonderful toys he wanted. Yes, Christmas was going to be great!

Chapter 1

20 DAYS BEFORE CHRISTMAS

Christmas was coming. Eve Dawson saw signs of it all around her Connecticut town as she walked home from work. Pine boughs and wreaths decorated front doors. Christmas lights and tempting gift displays adorned shopwindows. Even the snow blanketing lawns and rooftops and sitting in puffy mounds on all of the bushes looked festive. Yes, Christmas was coming, and with it, the anxiety of trying to squeeze a few extra dollars from her tight budget to buy presents for her five-year-old son, Harry.

The afternoon was growing dark as she hurried along. The shortened December days meant it was barely light when she left for work in the morning and nearly dark when she returned home. Harry would be watching for her from the picture window, eager to show her something he'd made in kindergarten or to talk about the latest exploits of his TV heroes, the Lone Ranger and Tonto. Eve remembered watching for her mum the same way, waiting outside Granny Maud's cottage for the first glimpse of Mum coming up the road. At least Eve's job in the typing pool allowed her to return home to Harry every day and tuck him into bed at night. When Eve was Harry's age, her mum, who'd also been a single mother, had worked as a live-in servant at Wellingford Hall and was only able to see Eve once a week.

A hunched figure hurried up the sidewalk toward Eve—Mrs. Herder, bundled against the cold and the gently falling snow, walking her dog. Eve smiled as they passed. "Hello. Lovely evening, isn't it?"

"If you like snow." Her words were muffled by the thick scarf wrapped around her neck and chin. Mrs. Herder continued past, her rambunctious yellow Labrador stopping to sniff at mailbox posts one minute, then tugging on his lead the next. They seemed a mismatched pair, the young dog too large and energetic for the small, white-haired woman who reminded Eve of her granny.

Eve quickened her steps, gazing at the houses she passed, wishing she had a home of her own for her and her son. What would that be like? Lights glowed from behind her neighbors' windows, revealing glimpses of their lives, as if peering at distant television screens. She knew very little about her neighbors, including Mrs. Herder, even though she passed the older woman and her dog nearly every day. Eve only assumed her name was Herder because it was printed on her mailbox out front. She lived in an historic house with a wide front porch that stood at the very edge of Eve's neighborhood of new, postwar bungalows. Mrs. Herder still displayed a gold star in her window six years after the war had ended, as if she didn't want anyone to forget that she had lost a loved one. The star stirred memories of Alfie Clarkson, Eve's first love, who had also died in the war. Alfie and Mum and Granny—Eve wished she could hang gold stars somewhere to tell the world how much she missed them.

She turned to watch Mrs. Herder and her dog walk up the steps and enter their house and felt a wave of homesickness for the English village of Wellingford, where she'd grown up. Her neighbors had known each other's names and had watched out for each other, their brick and stone cottages sitting shoulder to shoulder as if closing ranks against the outside world, not separated by private lawns and picket fences as they were here in America. The cottage in the village that she'd shared with Granny, and the nearby woods where she'd loved to roam, were the only true homes Eve could recall. But she had needed a new start for herself and Harry after the war, in a place where no one knew the shame of Harry's birth. While she wasn't proud of the way she had maneuvered that fresh start, things had turned out better than she deserved, for both her and her son. They lived with Eve's widowed friend, Audrey Barrett, paying rent every month, and the four of them had become a family of sorts. But if Eve could wish for any gift this Christmas, it would be a home of her own.

Harry wasn't in his usual place, watching for Eve from the front window as she walked up the driveway to Audrey's bungalow. She went inside through the kitchen door, stomping snow off her boots. She pulled off her hat, then smoothed down her hair. "It's snowing again," she told Audrey.

"The boys will be happy about that." Audrey stood at the kitchen stove, mashing a pot of potatoes into gooey submission. "Personally, I don't much like driving in snow."

"We drove our ambulances on some rather slippery roads during the war, remember?"

"At breakneck speed. With bombs falling. But it had to be done."

Eve hung up her coat and followed the happy sound of Harry's voice as he played with Audrey's son, Bobby. She found them sprawled on the rug in the living room, paging through a brightly colored catalogue. The boys were the same age and nearly the same size and might have been twins in their corduroy pants and plaid flannel shirts, except that Harry had ginger hair—a redhead, the Americans would say—and was friendly and talkative and boisterous. Bobby had inherited his father's ebony hair and his mother's shy reserve.

"What has you so charmed that you can't even say hello to your mum?" Eve asked.

"Hi, Mommy." Eve sighed inwardly at her son's American accent and wording. It was her own fault, since she had brought him to the States as an infant. Bobby, having been here for a year and a half, was starting to adopt the same type of speech, but at least he still called Audrey "Mummy."

Harry barely glanced up, as if he might miss something if he looked away for too long. "We're picking out all the toys we want Santa to bring us from the Christmas Wish Book." He pointed to the page, saying, "I want that airplane. Oooh, and that submarine, too! And I want this army truck and this tank and this motorcycle . . . We could play army, right, Bobby?"

"That would be fun!" Bobby laid his hand on the page for a moment as if claiming territory. "I want *all* of the trucks on this page—and especially this motorbus!"

Harry waited until his friend lifted his hand, then flipped to the next page. "I want this pickup truck. Look, it has lights that really light up! And wow, look at this steam shovel! We could dig holes with it!"

"I want one," Bobby said. "This army jeep has real lights, too!"

Eve squatted beside the boys for a better look as they continued turning pages, gleefully pointing to fire engines and bulldozers and police cars. "It looks to me like you're asking for every toy in the book."

"Not the *girls'* stuff," Harry said, making a face. "We don't want *dolls*!"

"Or baby toys," Bobby added. "Just the boys' toys on all of these pages." Eve watched them flip through a few more pages, chorusing, "I want this and this . . ."

She frowned. "There isn't room in this house for all of those toys. And besides, you have so many playthings already."

"But they're *old* toys, Mommy. These are *new* toys. We're going to ask Santa for all of these new toys when we see him at the parade tonight."

"The parade? That's tonight?"

"Yep. Did you forget, Mommy?"

"I may have, yes. I had a busy day at work." A mind-numbing day, actually. One that was exactly like the day before it and the one before that, clacking out letters in a windowless office as part of a typing pool. After paying her rent and a portion of the debt she felt she owed Audrey, Eve would be lucky to have enough money left over to buy one toy for Harry, let alone an entire catalogue full of them.

Audrey poked her head around the corner from the kitchen. "Dinner is ready. Wash up, please."

Eve stood and walked toward Audrey. "Where did they get the catalogue?"

"It's called the Wish Book, Mommy," Harry called to her.

"I think it came about a month ago, but I found it again when I straightened up this morning. They've been glued to it all afternoon." The boys stood to wash their hands, carrying the catalogue to the bathroom with them.

"Look at that, Bobby!" she heard Harry saying as they went. "It's a whole service station, with gasoline pumps and cars and everything!"

"I want one!"

"That Wish Book seems to have opened a Pandora's box of greedy longing," Eve told Audrey with a sigh.

When they finally sat down at the kitchen table, Harry bolted his food in record time. "Hurry, Mommy, hurry!" he begged. "We're gonna miss the Santa Claus Parade."

Eve continued to eat at a leisurely pace. "Don't worry. We have plenty of time."

"Do you have to go away tonight, Mummy?" Bobby asked Audrey. The worried look on his face was exactly like his mother's. Audrey had been a worrier for as long as Eve had known her, which was most of their thirty-two years. They had met as twelve-year-olds in the woods surrounding Wellingford Hall, where Eve's mother served as lady's maid to Audrey's mother, the wealthy and aristocratic Lady Rosamunde.

"No, my classes are all finished for the semester," Audrey replied.

"Don't you remember how anxious your mum was when she was studying for her exams last week?" Eve asked. "We barely got a full sentence out of her."

"My final marks came in the mail today," Audrey said quietly.

"Well, are you going to show us or were they a disaster?"

Audrey smiled her shy, Audrey smile, dipping her head as if bowing before royalty. "They weren't bad."

"Let me guess—you earned top marks in both classes, am I right?"

"Yes."

"Good job, you! We'll have to celebrate."

*　*　*

After eating, they stacked the supper dishes in the sink to save for later and bundled up for the short drive into town. On the way there, Eve heard the boys whispering in the backseat, and she swiveled around from the passenger seat to look. They had the catalogue open and were pointing and murmuring, "I want a gun and holster set like that!"

"We can pretend we're the Lone Ranger!"

"You brought the Wish Book with you? To a parade?" she asked in astonishment. The boys stared at her as if she'd asked a silly question.

"Did they really?" Audrey asked, glancing in the rearview mirror. "You've been studying it all afternoon, Bobby."

"I know, Mummy, but I might forget to tell Santa something I really, really want."

"We're gonna just *show* him everything instead," Harry added.

"You cannot sit on Santa's lap with the entire Sears Wish Book in your greedy little hands," Eve said.

"Why not?"

"Please, Mummy?"

"Well, for one thing, Santa Claus brings toys to a lot of other children besides you two," Eve said, "and the things you're asking for would fill his entire sleigh."

"He can make lots of trips, Mommy. He has all night."

Eve glanced at Audrey and saw her trying to hide a smile.

"Besides," Harry continued, "Santa only brings toys if you're good, and there are lots of kids at school who aren't being good."

"They'll get coal in their stockings," Bobby said solemnly.

Audrey found a parking spot near the village square, and as the boys tumbled out of the backseat, Eve spotted the catalogue peeking from beneath Harry's jacket. "The Wish Book stays in the car," she said, yanking it out and tossing it onto the seat.

"But, Mommy . . ."

She shut the car door. "If you can't remember everything on the list, maybe it's because your list is too long."

A huge Christmas tree stood in the picturesque town square, waiting for the mayor to throw the switch and light it up at the end of the parade.

"When are we going to get a Christmas tree?" Harry asked.

"Maybe this weekend. We'll cut one down from Uncle Tom's farm like we did last year, remember?"

Audrey's late husband's childhood friend Tom Vandenberg had been like a father to both of the boys, and he also held a special place in Eve's heart. In fact, he'd made it clear that he'd like to marry her and be more than just a father figure in Harry's life.

Beneath the village Christmas tree was a throne for Santa and a roped-off section where the children could form a queue to talk with him. Eve took Harry's hand in hers as they headed down the town's main street, wading through the crowd of pedestrians, searching for a place to stand along the parade route.

The quaint Connecticut town had been decorated with Christmas lights that twinkled against the snow, and the store windows were beautifully staged to tempt shoppers. Eve paused to look at a display of the latest aluminum kitchen appliances and coffeepots for modern housewives, along with aluminum ladders, Thermos bottles, and saws for their husbands. These were items that belonged in a home—a real home with a mother and father and children.

She closed her eyes, fighting off the familiar emptiness when she considered her and Audrey's makeshift family. At least Audrey had a respectable reason for being a single mum. And Eve should be thankful that her friend had invited Eve and Harry to share her home. She had lived off Audrey's insurance money and her husband's inheritance for nearly four years, living in Audrey's house, driving her car. And although Audrey wasn't demanding a penny of it, Eve was determined to pay it all back.

"Wow! Look at that airplane, Bobby!" Harry pointed to a large propeller plane, also made from aluminum, dangling behind the store window from a wire. "Was there a big airplane like that in the Wish Book?"

"I don't think so. I want it!"

"Me, too. We'll tell Santa tonight. What's the name of this store, Mommy? We need to tell Santa where he can buy it."

"Santa will know," Eve said, tugging his hand. "Come on."

No matter how far they walked, the sidewalks were so crowded with families and children standing three- and four-deep to watch the parade that Eve couldn't find a place where all of them could stand. The cadence of drums sounded in the distance. The parade was about to begin.

Harry hopped up and down in frustration. "I can't see! I can't see!"

"Mummy, look," Bobby said. "They have daddies to help them." He pointed to the families in front of them, and Eve saw that many of the fathers had lifted their small children onto their shoulders or held them in their arms so they could see. Eve and Audrey were both petite, and besides, the boys were too heavy to hold for the entire parade.

"I need a daddy so I can see," Harry told Eve. "Everyone else has one."

"It's not fair," Bobby pouted.

"Oh, dear," Eve murmured. She met Audrey's worried gaze.

The next moment, Harry dropped Eve's hand and ran up to a well-dressed gentleman who was just coming out of the department store. He carried a brightly wrapped box tied with a silver bow. "Will you be our daddy?" Harry asked him.

"Harry!" Eve gasped, horrified.

"Mine, too! Mine, too!" Bobby echoed, running to the man.

A tide of heat rushed to Eve's face as she hurried over to apologize to the gentleman and yank her son away. But before she could utter a sound, the man crouched down to talk to the boys. "Hello, Harry and Bobby. Are you here to see Santa Claus?" Eve recognized him then. Mr. Hamilton was the leader of their

Boys' Club at church. But she was still horribly embarrassed. And judging by her friend's expression, Audrey was too.

"Yeah. We were going to show Santa all the toys we wanted in the Wish Book," Harry told him, "but Mommy made us leave it in the car."

"I hope I can remember everything." Bobby wore his fretful look again.

Mr. Hamilton smiled. "I'm sure you'll remember the important things." He was probably in his midthirties and movie-star handsome. When millions of American GIs had landed in England during the war, Eve and Audrey and all the other women used to comment on how handsome the American men were—and here was another one, not wearing a uniform but a very expensive-looking overcoat, fedora, and cashmere scarf.

He stood again as the high school marching band approached playing "Jingle Bells."

"It's starting! The parade is starting!" Harry said, hopping up and down. "And we don't have a daddy!"

Mr. Hamilton gave Audrey and Eve a questioning look, as if not understanding.

"To boost them up," Eve said quickly, gesturing to the families around them.

"I see. I'll be glad to help." He handed his package to Audrey and crouched again, then lifted up both boys, one in each arm. Mr. Hamilton was a big man, tall and broad-shouldered, as solid as a Frigidaire. He looked as though he could easily manage two boys.

"But . . . I'm sure Mr. Hamilton needs to get home to his family and—" Audrey began.

"I don't mind at all," he said with a smile.

"Well . . . thank you. You can put them down whenever you get tired," Eve said.

Fire engines rolled past, red lights flashing. Prancing horses carried Roy Rogers and Hopalong Cassidy look-alikes shooting cap pistols. The mayor waved from inside a Model A Ford strung with fairy lights. Local business owners towed homemade floats with Christmas decorations and pretty high school girls singing carols. Santa's elves gave out candy canes to the children along the way. Then Santa Claus himself arrived, his sleigh pulled by a shiny new John Deere tractor.

"Hey! Where are all his reindeer?" Harry asked.

"Maybe they're resting up for their big night," Mr. Hamilton replied.

"They'll need a long rest after pulling a sleigh filled

with all the toys you boys want," Eve said. She and Audrey thanked Mr. Hamilton profusely when the parade ended and he had set the boys down on the sidewalk again. He tipped his hat to them and retrieved his package from Audrey.

"My pleasure, ladies. I hope you have a very merry Christmas—and that you boys get everything you want from that Wish Book."

"Not a chance," Eve mumbled. They followed the rest of the crowd back to the village square, applauding when the mayor flipped the switch and the towering Christmas tree lit up.

The queue of children waiting to sit on Santa's lap seemed miles long, and Eve was weary. The cold had seeped through her boots, chilling her toes. "It's going to take hours for you boys to have your turn," she moaned. "And then another hour to recite the unabridged version of the Wish Book to him."

"I have an idea," Audrey said. "Why don't you write letters to Santa instead? That way, you can take your time, and you won't forget anything." Audrey's cheeks were as red as apples, and she was shivering. The boys seemed oblivious to the cold.

"But I can't write yet, Mummy. Just my name."

"I'll help you. I promise."

"That's a great idea," Eve said. "Let's go home."

"He's only Santa's helper, anyway," she heard Harry telling Bobby as they trudged back to the car. "The real Santa lives at the North Pole and has lots and lots of toys to make."

* * *

Harry got into a tug-of-war with Bobby at bedtime, arguing over which of them would get to sleep with the Wish Book under his pillow. "It isn't going under either one of your pillows," Audrey said, taking it away. "It's not as though you've lost a tooth and are waiting for the tooth fairy." She set the book on their dresser for the night.

"But, Mummy . . . ," Bobby whined.

"Didn't you see all of those other children at the parade tonight?" Eve asked. "Santa has to bring presents to them, too. He can't bring you every single toy in the Wish Book."

"We'll ask Nana and Granddad for the rest," Eve heard Harry say as she switched off the light. "They always buy lots and lots of presents." Eve started to argue but knew it was true. She looked at Audrey helplessly.

Eve went into the kitchen with Audrey afterwards, talking while they washed and dried the dishes. "I wasn't familiar with all of the American Christmas traditions last year," Audrey said as she rinsed suds off a plate. "But I do remember that my in-laws gave Bobby a great many toys, and it did seem a bit too much. I guess I was so overwhelmed by the love Robert's parents showed Bobby and me that I didn't want to speak up about all the toys."

"I'm quite sure Nana Barrett will repeat her performance this Christmas. She does it every year." Eve and Harry had spent every Christmas with the Barretts since Harry was a baby, and while she still felt uncomfortable with the extravagant generosity, she had come to expect it. Harry, of course, didn't have any problem with it at all. Until last year, Eve had allowed the Barretts to believe she and Harry were their daughter-in-law and grandson, and it was only by God's grace that they still wanted to maintain a close relationship with Eve after she confessed her deception.

"Even if the Barretts can afford every toy in the Wish Book," Audrey said, "I don't want Bobby to grow up craving so many things—or expecting to get them. It isn't right."

Eve wiped a plate dry and put it in the cupboard. "I remember being grateful for just a few simple gifts at Christmas when I was their age. I would hang my stocking on my bedpost for Father Christmas to fill, and in the morning, I'd find a doll or a toy on top . . . maybe an orange and some candy. Granny would knit new mittens or a hat for me. I learned later that Mum had saved up for months to buy me those things. She always had to work on Christmas Day, but we could spend Boxing Day together." Eve wondered if her mum had felt the same sense of loss at missing out on her child's life because of her need to work.

"I remember how our gardener would cut armloads of greens and holly branches," Audrey said, her hands submerged in the soapy dishwater. "Wellingford Hall looked and smelled so splendid. There would be a huge tree and presents to unwrap, chosen by my tutor, Miss Blake, I'm sure. Not by my parents. And we always had Christmas crackers to pop open at the table. But best of all, Alfie would be home from boarding school for a few weeks."

They worked in silence, Audrey scrubbing a pot with

a Brillo pad. Eve supposed they were both remembering Audrey's older brother, Alfie, and how much they had both loved him. "During the war," Audrey said, "we were grateful if we got through Christmas without being startled out of our beds in the middle of the night by air-raid sirens, remember?"

"Oh yes. And I remember how the American GIs would hold sprigs of mistletoe over our heads at the Christmas dances so they could steal a kiss."

Audrey fell silent again, and Eve knew she was thinking of her husband, Robert. "I want Harry to have lovely memories of Christmas, but I don't think getting every toy in the Wish Book is going to accomplish it. Besides, I can't spend wads of money on presents with my budget."

"My brother felt entitled to anything and everything he ever wished for, and it ruined him in the end. I don't want that to happen to Bobby. Is there some way we can teach them not to want so much?" Audrey handed Eve the pot to dry and pulled the stopper from the sink.

"I don't know. I'll have to think about it. But I agree. They need to learn that Christmas is more than getting every toy they could ever wish for." She finished drying the pot and put it away. "That was nice of their Boys' Club leader to help us tonight, wasn't it?"

"Oh, but I was so embarrassed! And I'm worried, Eve. The boys are starting to notice that the other children have fathers and they don't."

"There's at least one other family at church who lost their father during the war."

"That isn't the point, really. It's a father's role that's missing from their lives. Even for simple things like a ride on his shoulders. We both know what it's like to grow up without a father's love, and now our sons will know it, too."

"They have Tom Vandenberg. He's been like a father to them." Eve was sorry she'd mentioned Tom the moment the words were out of her mouth.

"Do you think you'll marry him someday?" Audrey asked. "I can tell that he loves you."

"I don't know." Eve shrugged as if it didn't matter. But it did. "Are you going to get married again so Bobby can have a father?"

Audrey looked away. "Let's go to bed."

Chapter 2

Audrey stood at the kitchen window, staring out at the snow-covered back garden, her cup of tea untouched and turning cold. The thought of this morning's appointment made her stomach jittery. Was she really ready to take such a huge step? She and her son had already experienced so many changes, and she had always hated change.

Though Bobby had been too young to know the difference, their lives had been upended on that day more than five years ago when she received their immigration papers. Within hours, she'd also received a telegram from her father-in-law saying that Robert had been killed in a car accident. Unable to face coming to America without her husband to welcome her, she'd chosen to stay home at Wellingford Hall.

Then, just a year and a half ago, her father had shocked her with the announcement that she was the product of one of her mother's extramarital affairs and therefore he was disowning both her and her son. With no other options, she had finally come to America, to Robert's family. And even more surprises and changes had greeted her here.

No, Audrey didn't need any more change. Perhaps she should think this new step through a bit more, wait a bit longer. Besides, the roads were snow-covered. Surely she could wait another day. Or a week.

She watched as Eve rummaged through her coat pockets, searching for something. "What did I do with my gloves?" she asked. "I'm going to miss my bus and be late for work."

"You can borrow mine." Audrey went to the coat hooks and took a pair from her pockets. She checked on the boys to make sure they were eating their breakfast and saw the Wish Book spread open between them on the kitchen table. Their neglected Rice Krispies were congealing in soggy lumps that no longer went snap, crackle, and pop. Audrey scooped the catalogue off the table and set it on top of the Frigidaire. "No time for that nonsense now."

"You said we could write a letter to Santa since we didn't get to sit on his lap last night," Bobby said.

"And we will. After school. Now please eat, or you'll miss your bus, too."

Eve had already left, but here she was back again, sticking her head into the kitchen. "By the way, you're still going to the bank today, right, Audrey? You're not going to turn coward on me at the last minute, are you?"

"Well . . . actually . . . the roads are slippery and—"

Eve hurried inside again, leaving the door open. "We had a pact, Audrey. You said if you did well in school this semester, you would enroll in college full-time next fall. I can take time off and go to the bank with you if—"

"No, no . . . get going," she said, pushing Eve toward the door. "I'm perfectly capable of going on my own."

"I know you're capable, but *will* you go? Today?"

"I will. As soon as the boys are on their way." Whether she was frightened or not, she would go. After all, the bank might turn down her request for a loan, and then she could rethink her plans.

* * *

An hour later, Audrey was feeling jittery again as she opened the massive door to enter the savings and loan. The bank on the village's main street was a huge, cavernous place, its marble grandeur mimicking a temple to an ancient Greek god. If it had been designed to make Audrey feel small and insignificant, it was succeeding. The enormous Christmas tree that stood in the center of the lobby and the tinsel garlands spiraling up the imposing pillars did little to soften the effect. Audrey still felt a bit like the Cowardly Lion approaching the great and terrible Wizard of Oz. Her boots echoed on the marble floor as she crossed to speak to the receptionist. "Good morning, I'm Mrs. Barrett. I have an appointment to speak with a loan officer?"

"Yes, he's expecting you, Mrs. Barrett. Right this way."

Audrey peered inside the vault as she passed it, marveling at the thickness of the door and wondering what treasures lay inside the dozens of safety-deposit boxes.

When she turned to follow the receptionist again, there stood Mr. Hamilton—the leader of Bobby's Boys' Club at church and stand-in father from the parade. She felt the blood rush to her face.

"Oh! H-hello, Mr. Hamilton."

"Good to see you again, Mrs. Barrett." He shook her hand as the receptionist slipped away. "Please, come inside my office and have a seat." He left a trail of cologne in his wake as he helped her with her coat and showed her to a chair. He was a ridiculously attractive man with thick, wavy blond hair that he combed back from his broad face and an impertinent dimple in his cheek when he smiled. Audrey noticed the fine quality of his tailored suit, crisply starched shirt, and expensive silk tie. Even the matching silk pocket-square peeking from his suit coat looked perfect.

Mr. Hamilton's clothes and demeanor triggered an avalanche of memories, burying Audrey beneath prewar images of endless dinners at posh establishments, dancing to string orchestras with languid, boring men who took their upper-class life entirely for granted. Audrey's mother, the daughter of an earl, had been determined that Audrey find a "suitable match." How thankful Audrey was that instead, she'd found a kind and loving husband in Robert, someone who shared her dreams and goals.

"I see you survived the Santa Claus Parade," Mr. Hamilton said. The images vanished, leaving only the memory of last night's embarrassment after her son had asked this man to be his father.

"Ehm . . . yes. Thank you for taking time to help the boys last night. It was very kind of you."

"Bobby's a great kid. He was a little shy around the other boys in the club, at first—quite the opposite of his friend Harry. But he's starting to participate more."

"He enjoys it so much. Eve and I are happy they have a chance to be with other boys their age and with . . ." *With a male role model.* Audrey didn't finish.

Mr. Hamilton broke the awkward silence. "I knew your husband, Mrs. Barrett. Everyone in town knew Bob, in fact. I'm so sorry for your loss. And for Bobby's, too. It was a terrible tragedy."

"Thank you." Audrey hoped he would change the subject, but he continued on.

"I was a year ahead of him in school, but the Famous Four, as he and his group of friends were called, dominated every sport from baseball to basketball. I played football with them. The American game, not what you British folk call football."

"Yes. I understand that it's an entirely different game."

"I was one of the big guys who tackled our opponents. Bob was the quarterback. He had a powerful throwing arm."

Audrey cleared the knot from her throat, angry with herself for still getting emotional whenever someone talked about Robert. She wanted to change the subject. "Do you have a kindergartner, too? Is that why you're leading their Boys' Club group?"

"I'm not married. The church is always looking for leaders, so I volunteered because I enjoyed Boys' Club myself as a boy."

"How lovely. Ehm . . . perhaps we should get down to business?" she said, clearing her throat again. "I wanted to explain why I'm applying for this loan. It's a bit complicated, you see—"

"Maybe I can spare you by saying that I already know a bit about you. You're British, which is obvious from your charming accent—and I understand that Bob married you when he was stationed over there during the war."

"I was still in England when I received the news about his accident, and so I decided to remain there. In the meantime, my friend Eve Dawson . . . well . . ."

"This is a small town, Mrs. Barrett, and I golf at the country club. Everyone knows what happened."

"Believe me, it's all in the past now. Eve and I are sharing the house Robert built for me and working together to raise our sons."

"Not everyone would be as forgiving as you've been."

"Eve is my best friend." Audrey's voice turned sharp, her words clipped. "I won't say anything bad about her. And I have no patience with anyone who does speak ill of her."

"I'm sorry. I didn't mean—"

"What Eve and I would both like very much to do is to put it all behind us and start over again. We considered moving to a different town where no one knows us, but we felt it would be unfair to Robert's parents to take their grandsons away. They consider Harry every bit as much their grandson as Bobby. They've been very generous to Eve and me."

"I admire your courage for picking up stakes to start over in a new country."

"Yes, well, neither of us had a choice, really. Anyway,

since you already know the details of my situation, let's talk about the loan, shall we?" She knew she sounded cold and stiff, but there was something about his expensive suit and the casual way he talked about golfing at the country club that put her off.

"Of course." He folded his hands on the desk and waited as if afraid to speak and offend her again.

"I plan to pursue a degree in nursing, and I would like to attend the junior college full-time in the fall once Bobby is in school all day. The loan would cover my tuition and other expenses for the two-year program. I plan to repay the loan after I graduate and find a job."

"How did you become interested in nursing?" The question threw her off stride for a moment.

"Eve and I enlisted in the Auxiliary Territorial Service during the war and drove ambulances. We were taught the basics of first aid, and I found I quite liked helping people. I believe it will be a suitable career that will allow me to support my son and myself in the future."

He looked at her for what seemed like a very long time without speaking. She found it unnerving not to know what he was thinking. She could only imagine that he, like most other men, disapproved of careers for women with small children.

When his silence became awkward, she pulled the papers she'd brought with her from her purse. "I have the deed to the home Robert built for me, which I hope to use as collateral. The home is mortgage-free and the deed is in my name. This second page shows the combined fees for tuition and other expenses, such as textbooks and laboratory fees, for the two-year nursing program." She slid the papers across the desk, and when Mr. Hamilton leaned forward to take them, she got another whiff of his cologne. Her longing for Robert nearly overwhelmed her. "You'll see that I've listed the starting salary for nurses at the regional hospital and for other places that are currently hiring nurses."

"You're very thorough." He laid the papers down and folded his hands on his desk again. "Forgive me if I'm being too forward, Mrs. Barrett, but I know your husband's father quite well. My family and his have done business together at this bank for years. My grandfather was one of its founders, and the Barretts were principal investors. The trust fund they set up for Robert, which I understand belongs to you and your son now, is administered through this bank."

"I'm aware of that. It's why I came to this bank first."

"Then you must know that there's no need to mortgage your home. Surely your husband's family would sponsor your education with an interest-free loan?"

Audrey looked away for a moment. "I had hoped not to go into this . . . but I'm afraid the Barretts don't understand my desire for a career. Especially in a field like nursing, which they consider common and undignified."

"They said that?"

She stared at her lap, remembering her father-in-law's words and the rejection she'd felt as he'd dismissed her aspirations with a wave of his hand. She also remembered driving to the devastated city of Coventry after a night of relentless Nazi bombing and offering badly needed help to its suffering people. She could have stayed safe in Wellingford Hall that morning, but she had vowed not to turn away from need, to make her life count.

"Mr. Barrett expressed his displeasure when I mentioned nursing and was quick to point out that none of the other young mothers at your country club have careers. I think he and Mrs. Barrett are hoping I'll change my mind and settle down to live off their very generous trust fund. But I have no wish to fill my days with shopping trips and luncheons and tennis matches."

There was something in Mr. Hamilton's expression that Audrey couldn't interpret, almost as if he was trying not to smile. It made her furious. "Robert and I made many plans for how we would live after the war, and neither of us wanted a life of pointless leisure. Like Robert, I was also raised with wealth and privilege, and my experience was that it was an empty life. During the war, everyone worked together to help save England, rich and poor alike, and no job was too demeaning. I felt I finally was able to make a contribution and do some good in this world."

"Your mother-in-law is involved with several charities—"

"Mrs. Barrett may do whatever she likes with her money. I didn't earn the money that's sitting in your bank in my name, Mr. Hamilton. Besides, I want to serve people with my own two hands, face-to-face, not by writing a cheque. Robert would be very disappointed in me if I adopted the leisurely life that he had decided to break away from. It was our intent to be independent of family wealth. To work hard and make our own way. To teach our son to work hard."

"I see."

She could tell nothing from his expression. "I'm afraid my words are coming out all wrong, and I'm giving the impression that I'm judging the Barretts and condemning the way they live. If so, please forgive me. That's not at all what I intended. It's just that I want to make my own choices, and this is what I've chosen to do."

"I understand."

Did he? Audrey wondered if she'd overstepped some invisible boundary and had been too strident and judgmental, as if she'd been trying to change Mr. Hamilton to her way of thinking. She drew a breath to calm herself. "I'm sure you're very busy, and here I am going on and on. You don't need to hear all the reasons behind my decisions but simply to know that I would like to apply for a loan using my home as collateral." Then another thought occurred to her. "I never considered that you may not wish to damage your bank's relationship with Mr. Barrett by giving me a loan behind his back, so to speak. I'll understand if that's the case, and I'll apply at a different bank—"

"I assure you that won't be a problem." He opened his mouth as if to say more, then hesitated for a long moment. "May I just say, Mrs. Barrett . . . I am very impressed and amazed by your resolve. You've faced unimaginable suffering without self-pity, and you know beyond any doubt what you want in life. Not many people our age have that much insight. I admire your courage and your determination, and I wish you well. With your career and with raising your son. He's fortunate to have such a remarkable mother."

"You're kind to say so." She felt the heat in her cheeks again. "Now, about the loan . . . ?"

"I'll be happy to approve your application. I'll put it through myself, in fact." He bent to open a drawer in his desk and pulled out some papers. "The first step is to fill out this standard form. Later on, the bank will require a home inspection to assess the value of your property. It won't be much of a hurdle since I understand you live in a newer home in a nice neighborhood."

Audrey wondered how he knew where she lived. "Thank you. I'm very grateful for your help, Mr. Hamilton."

He slid the papers and a pen over to her side of the desk. "I'll start the rest of the paperwork while you fill this out. And don't worry about the bottom part where it says, 'other assets.' We have your trust fund figures on file."

"Will this paperwork take long? Bobby and Harry are due home from kindergarten a little before noon." And she had no desire to stay in Mr. Hamilton's office a moment longer than necessary.

"Just write in your personal information and I'll do the rest. We'll need your signature, but that can come later."

She finished several minutes later and passed the papers back to him. "Am I done for today?"

"Yes." They both stood, and he reached to shake her hand. "It's been a pleasure, Mrs. Barrett." He came around the desk to help her with her coat. "I see that it's snowing again. I imagine you don't often get this much snow in London."

"Not often, no." London seemed very far away at the moment, as if it were a place she had only dreamt about.

* * *

Audrey made it home in plenty of time before the boys' school bus arrived. She took off her hat and changed from her suit into slacks and a sweater. When she glanced at herself in the mirror, she noticed that Eve had tucked the letter with her college marks in a prominent place beneath the frame. *We need to celebrate!* she'd scribbled on the envelope.

Audrey smiled. Eve was such a good friend, encouraging her studies and cheering her success. Audrey hadn't been entirely certain that she could return to school after all these years, wondering if she could even do the work and if she would feel awkward to be in class again at age thirty-two. But there were other adult students at the junior college, mostly men studying on the GI bill.

Tears filled her eyes, and she had to sit down on the edge of the bed. Robert was supposed to be sharing this bungalow with her and their son. They were supposed to be pursuing their dreams together. When the war ended and she'd kissed Robert goodbye before he shipped home, she'd never imagined that she was kissing him and holding him for the last time. He had made her feel cherished and adored for the first time in her life, and she feared she would never feel that way again.

She drew a ragged breath and stood. The boys would be home soon. She must pull herself together and fix lunch. She reached to wipe her tears and noticed that her hand still carried the lingering scent of Mr. Hamilton's cologne from shaking his hand. She went into the bathroom and scrubbed it off.

Audrey was making grilled cheese sandwiches when the boys clomped through the door, their galoshes dripping water on the linoleum, their wet mittens and snow pants piling up in a sodden, untidy heap.

"Hang everything up on the hooks, please," she told them.

Bobby tugged her apron afterwards. "Can we have the book now, Mummy?"

"What book?"

"The Wish Book." He pointed to the top of the Frigidaire, where she'd put it that morning. "You promised we would write a letter to Santa Claus, remember?"

"Did the mailman come yet?" Harry asked. "Is it too late to mail it?"

"There are still nineteen days until Christmas. You'll have plenty of time to write and mail your letters."

Bobby tugged her apron again. "But can we have the book now?"

"After lunch. And then I think you should narrow down your list to a few favorite toys. You don't want Santa to think you're greedy, do you?"

"But, Mummy, they're *all* my favorites!"

She exhaled. This was getting out of control. She regretted that they'd ever found the Wish Book in the first place. She turned to get milk from the refrigerator and heard Harry say in a low voice, "We'll show Nana the book. She'll buy us everything."

Audrey recalled her conversation with Mr. Hamilton at the bank. She'd gotten through to him and made him understand her thoughts about overindulgence and managing wealth, but the bigger job would be to make the Barretts understand. And Bobby. She and Eve had been trying to do that by giving the boys chores to do and a small weekly allowance. But the unchecked flow of toys from Nana would have to stop. Audrey pulled out a kitchen chair and sat down at the table to face them.

"Listen, you two. Nana isn't going to buy you everything in the Wish Book. I don't want to hear you pestering her, either."

"Why not?" Bobby asked.

"It's Christmas," Harry added. "She always buys lots of toys for Christmas."

"Because we don't demand gifts from Santa or Nana

or anyone else, even when they're as generous as Nana is. Christmas is about more than getting presents."

"Like what?" Bobby asked.

Audrey had no idea where to begin. She and Eve would need to come up with a plan. And soon! "We'll finish this conversation when Harry's mum gets home. Now, eat your lunch before your sandwiches get cold."

They nodded solemnly and bit into their cheese sandwiches. But when Audrey returned to the kitchen after going outside to empty the rubbish bin, she saw that they had scraped a chair over to the refrigerator and rescued the Wish Book.

After lunch she found the boys inside a fort they'd constructed on their bottom bunk, half-hidden beneath a tent of blankets. They had the Wish Book open to the toy section and were whispering, "I want this army set . . . oooh, and these Lincoln Logs, too . . ."

Chapter 3

On Saturday morning, Eve and Audrey lured Harry and Bobby away from *Sky King* and their other television shows to drive out to Tom Vandenberg's farm to cut down a Christmas tree. Eve loved the farm and the rolling countryside, which looked quaint and charming beneath a blanket of fresh snow. It had always reminded her of the rural area in England where she had grown up, first living in a cottage with Granny Maud and later as a servant at Wellingford Hall, Audrey's family's great manor house.

Granny loved telling stories about how Eve's daddy,

who had died before Eve was born, used to tend his flock of sheep on the farm. Sometimes one of them would squeeze under the fence and wander away. And Daddy would go looking for it, bringing it home just like the shepherd in the story Jesus told. Eve had seen Tom care for his newborn lambs the same way.

Silvery icicles dangled from the roof of the farmhouse like jewels. Sheep in their thick winter coats waddled in the snowy barnyard, while black-and-white cows lined up along the fence, a brown-eyed welcoming committee. The woods beyond the farm had been Eve's refuge, and Tom her closest friend, during the years when she had pretended to be Audrey. Harry called Tom's parents Grandma and Grandpa Van. His mother had become like a second mother to Eve. Thankfully, Eve's friendship with the Vandenbergs had survived after she'd confessed, but she still felt a cloud of shame following her and darkening her way forward.

Her sins were piled a mile high—the adultery that had led to Harry's conception, the way she'd deceived everyone she had come to love in America, and the money she'd stolen from Audrey during the years she and Harry had lived off the life insurance and trust fund that Robert Barrett had intended for his family.

Tom and his mother both assured her that God would forgive her if she asked Him to. She *had* asked, and she knew He had. Just as the Vandenbergs and Barretts—and even Audrey—had done. Tom said that once Jesus took away her guilt, she could start all over again. God forgave and forgot Eve's past. If only Eve could fully forgive herself and forget how she had hurt the people who meant the most to her. Paying back Audrey's money was her way of facing the consequences for the wrongs she had done.

The boys leaped from the backseat of the car to run to Tom as he emerged from the barn with a long wooden sled. "Is that for us, Uncle Tom? Is the sled for us?" Harry asked, bouncing up and down.

Tom crouched to show it to them. "Yep. This sled was mine when I was a boy. Your father used to ride it, too, Bobby. I just finished waxing the runners, so it should glide like the wind."

Kind, patient Tom had been one of Robert Barrett's closest friends and a man Eve knew she could always rely on. She gazed across the pasture at the distant trees and inhaled the fresh country air. Whenever she came here after a hectic week at work, she felt as though she could breathe again. The farmhouse, always warm and cozy inside, was more than 150 years old in its oldest sections, and it was filled with comfortable furnishings, family heirlooms, and mementos from generations of Vandenbergs. It felt more like home to Eve than the bungalow she shared with Audrey, and yet it seemed wrong for her to ever consider it her home. Each time she visited, her heart was torn between her longing to enjoy this farm and the people she loved, and her guilt in knowing that she didn't deserve such contentment.

"I thought you boys might like to go sledding before we picked out your Christmas tree," Tom said. "That hill over there is the perfect place for it." He stood again and turned to Eve and Audrey. "Would that be okay with you ladies?"

"I'm sure they would love it," Audrey replied.

"I think my mom has plans to feed them afterwards," he added.

"That sounds wonderful," Eve said.

"I want a sled for Christmas!" Harry said as they tromped through snowdrifts to the sledding hill.

"Me, too! Me, too!" Bobby said.

"We didn't write our letters to Santa Claus yet, so let's add sleds to our list."

"Write down two sleds," Bobby told his mother. "Okay? Don't forget." Eve looked at Audrey and rolled her eyes.

"You're making a list for Santa Claus, huh?" Tom asked.

"We're picking out all the toys we want from this." Bobby stopped walking and pulled the Sears Wish Book from inside his jacket.

Eve groaned. She had frisked Harry before leaving the house but didn't think to check Bobby.

"You brought it with you?" Audrey asked. "I don't believe it! Such cheek!"

"They want everything in the toy section," Eve explained to Tom. "It's getting a little out of hand."

Bobby yanked off his mittens to show the catalogue to Tom, who squatted down to see. It fell open to the toys.

"We want rifles like these for Christmas," Harry said. "They shoot corks for bullets."

"And we want the gun and holster set on the next page, too," Bobby added.

"You have the book *memorized*?" Eve widened her eyes in disbelief.

Tom patiently studied the pages as the boys chattered

on and on about rifles and cap pistols with leather holsters.

"Will you teach us to shoot, Uncle Tom?" Harry asked. "You know how to shoot because you were in the war, right?"

Tom stood without replying. He never talked about the war or about being wounded in Italy. "Hey, I forgot to ask," he said. "How was the Christmas parade the other night?"

"Very bad, at first," Harry said. "We needed a daddy."

"So we asked Mr. Hamilton to be ours," Bobby said.

Tom gave Eve a questioning look.

"Mr. Hamilton was kind enough to lift them up so they could see over everyone's heads," she explained. "He's their Boys' Club leader at church, and he happened to come along at the right time."

Harry tugged Tom's hand. "Maybe you could be my daddy next time, Uncle Tom, so Mr. Hamilton wouldn't have to hold both of us. Please?"

Eve held her breath, dreading Tom's answer. Again, he didn't reply as he continued walking toward the sledding hill on the other side of the farmhouse. He whistled for his dog, who came bounding over, tail wagging. "There you are, Champ. You forgot to say hello to Harry and Bobby."

Eve pulled the Wish Book from Bobby's hands as the boys fell all over the friendly mutt, hugging and petting him. Their jackets would smell like a wet dog afterwards, but they both loved romping with him. She was relieved that the conversation had been diverted from her son needing a daddy, but then Harry suddenly said, "What I really, *really* want for Christmas is a dog."

"Let's ask Santa for one!" Bobby said.

Eve met Audrey's gaze, shaking her head in frustration. Tom's dog followed them to the top of the rise, jumping and frolicking while Tom loaded the boys onto his sled. After showing Harry how to steer, he gave the sled a running start and a hearty push, and down the hill they went, laughing and whooping. The dog raced behind them, barking and prancing, then it panted back up the hill with them as they pulled the sled to the top.

"Let me steer this time," Bobby said.

"Such boundless energy," Eve marveled.

Eventually, after several trips up and down the hill, the boys were tuckered out. Their snow pants were soaked; their cheeks glowed. Tom loaded them onto the sled again and pulled them across the pasture to the edge of the woods in search of a Christmas tree. Eve inhaled the scent of pine carried on the breeze. "I always hate the thought of cutting down a tree," she said. "It's a living thing that took years to grow."

"I know," Tom said, grinning. "You tell me that every year." He turned to Audrey. "And every year I tell her that my great-grandfather started this grove just for Christmas trees. He would plant a half-dozen new ones every year so our family would always have a supply."

"It takes foresight to be thinking that far into the future," Audrey said.

"Buying a tree from a lot just isn't the same as cutting one yourself and bringing it home," Tom said. "I've continued the tradition. I planted these last year." He gestured to a row of trees barely three feet tall. "For my grandchildren, I hope." He looked at Eve when he said it. His hand rested gently on Harry's head. Eve had to turn away before the love she saw in Tom's eyes swallowed her whole.

They walked through the grove of trees for several minutes, analyzing each tree, trying to choose the perfect one. Harry stopped beside one that was taller than Tom by at least two feet. "We need this big, *big* tree,

Uncle Tom, so there will be room for lots and lots of presents under it."

"It's much too big for our little bungalow," Eve said. "We'd never get it through the door, and even then it would scrape the ceiling." Most of the other trees the boys chose were also too big, but at last Tom helped them select a lovely Scotch pine that seemed just the right size.

"Can we help you chop it down, Uncle Tom?" Harry asked.

"We'll be careful," Bobby added.

"I don't know . . . This ax is pretty heavy," he replied, much to Eve's relief. "Maybe next year, okay? I'll bring a hatchet that's more your size."

Eve's toes felt frozen by the time Tom finished chopping down the tree and loading it onto the sled for the trip back to the farmhouse. "I think Grandma Van has chicken noodle soup and hot chocolate inside," he told the boys when they reached the farmyard. Eve started to follow them but Tom stopped her. "Eve, wait. Can we talk?"

She feared she knew what was coming.

Tom chewed his lip, staring at the ground as if searching for a place to begin, before looking up at her again.

"Eve, it makes me so frustrated to hear Harry talking about wanting a dad. You know how I feel about you. I would like nothing more than to be Harry's dad and your husband. And unless you've changed your mind for some reason, I'm pretty sure you love me, too."

Eve did love him. And her heart ached from holding the words inside every time she saw Tom. "You know why I can't get serious with you," she said instead. "Not yet. Not until I've paid back all the money I spent when I was pretending to be Audrey."

"That was more than a year ago. Surely you've paid that debt by now."

"Hardly! Not on my secretary's salary. I lived off Audrey's insurance money for four years."

"She isn't demanding it, is she? How long are you going to punish yourself?"

"There are still plenty of people in this town who know what I've done. I can't bring my shame to you and your family until I make up for it and prove that I'm not a bad person."

"It doesn't matter to me what people think. It shouldn't matter to you, either."

"Besides, Audrey needs my help. I owe her that much. The boys will be in school all day next year, and she's going to take college courses full-time. I need to help with the household expenses and the chores and taking care of the boys—"

"Excuses, Eve. And not very good ones." He lifted the tree off the sled and hefted it onto the roof of Audrey's car. "You can still keep working to repay Audrey after we're married, if that's what you think you need to do. And we could both help her with Bobby. I want to be with you. All the time." He pulled Eve close, and she laid her head on his chest. He smelled of pine and the outdoors. She loved being in his arms and was continually amazed that Tom knew all about her—not only her lies and deceptions, but also that she'd had Harry out of wedlock, fathered by a married man, no less. And yet Tom loved her. Forgave her.

"Eve, if you love me—"

"We need to wait, Tom."

He released her. "I'm tired of waiting. Tired of excuses."

The hurt expression on his face brought tears to her eyes. She turned away so he wouldn't see them. And so that she wouldn't change her mind. "I'm sorry, Tom, but I have to do this on my own." She hurried toward the farmhouse, hoping he wouldn't follow, feeling relieved when he didn't. She paused on the enclosed porch to compose herself before going into the kitchen.

Audrey sat at the table sipping hot chocolate with the boys, who were showing Grandma Vandenberg the Wish Book. Harry looked up as Eve came inside, and she saw that he was sporting a chocolate mustache. "We found the sled we want, Mommy. Look! It's right here in the Wish Book."

If only the Wish Book could grant wishes for grown-ups, too.

"But they don't have dogs," Bobby said. "We looked and looked."

"Dogs aren't toys, and they don't like being stuffed into Santa's toy sack." Eve's irritation was evident in her voice. She felt Grandma Van studying her but couldn't meet her gaze.

Grandma Van gently closed the Wish Book and rose to ladle soup into the waiting bowls. "Do you boys know why we celebrate Christmas?" she asked as she worked.

"Because that's when Santa Claus comes and brings toys," Harry replied.

"That's one tradition, but Christmas is much more

than that. It's Jesus' birthday. We celebrate the day He was born just like we celebrate your birthdays."

Eve ruffled her son's sweaty red hair as she sank onto a chair beside him. The bowl of soup Grandma Van set in front of her smelled heavenly.

"You boys know the story of baby Jesus in the manger, don't you?" Grandma Van continued.

"We colored a picture of it in Sunday school," Bobby said.

"Bobby and I knew what a manger was because there's one in your barn for the sheep."

Grandma Van smiled. "Jesus was God's Son, but when He was born, He didn't even have a place to stay or a crib to sleep in. Only a stable and a manger."

"We're going to be in a play about baby Jesus in school," Bobby said.

"We're gonna wear costumes and everything. We're the smart kings."

Grandma Van looked puzzled for a moment, then chuckled. "You mean the Wise Men?"

"Yep. We get to wear gold crowns because we're the *rich* smart kings with lots and lots of gold."

"Then you must know that the kings were bringing the gold as a gift for baby Jesus for His birthday. God gave Jesus to us as a gift because He loves us. And now we give gifts to the people we love at Christmas."

"Can you and Grandpa and Uncle Tom come and see us in the play, Grandma Van?"

"Of course, sweetie pie. Let me know when it is and we'll be there."

* * *

Tom had tied the Christmas tree to the roof of Audrey's car with ropes, and once they reached home, it took both Eve and Audrey, pushing and tugging, to get it off the car and shoved to the side of the driveway. They couldn't lug the prickly thing an inch farther. "Rather like maneuvering a gigantic hedgehog, isn't it?" Eve asked with a sigh. Worn-out, they left the tree lying in the snowbank beside the driveway for now.

After supper, they all sat down in the living room together with the Wish Book open to the toy section so the boys could write their letters to Santa Claus. Harry bent close, his nose inches from the stationery as he watched Eve write.

"Can we send a letter to Nana, too?" he asked, looking up.

"We already talked about not pestering Nana, remember? Didn't you hear what Grandma Van explained today, about how Christmas is Jesus' birthday?"

"But how will Nana know what to buy if we don't send her a list?"

Eve sighed. "I'm sure she will manage. Let's get on with it, shall we?"

"Okay. I want this toy steam shovel. It really scoops up dirt."

"Me, too," Bobby said. "Make sure you write down the page number, Mummy, so Santa can find it faster."

"How many pages are there?" Audrey wet her finger and flipped through page after page of the toy section. "Listen, maybe you should choose just one toy from each page."

"Mummy, no! What if there are lots of good things on the same page?"

"Then you'll have to choose the best one."

Harry flopped over onto the floor as if he'd been shot. "That's impossible! We have everything picked out already!"

Eve laid down her pen. "Then I suggest you take some time to carefully choose again. The letters can wait one more day." Harry drummed his feet on the floor in frustration. "And if you keep that up," Eve added, "the only thing Santa will bring you is a sack full of coal." The drumming stopped.

"Mummy, can I show you one thing we want that's not on the toy pages?" Bobby asked.

Audrey tilted her head. "I suppose."

Eve watched as Bobby turned to the menswear section in the front of the catalogue, where a corner of the page had been folded down. He pointed to a man's suit. "We want this, Mummy."

"Those suits won't fit you. They're for grown men. But they probably have suits in your size in the boy's department—"

"Not the clothes, Mummy—the daddy. I want a daddy. For all the parades."

"We can share the same one if he's big and strong like Mr. Hamilton," Harry said. "And if he can pick us both up at the same time."

"We need him to live here with us so he can carry our Christmas tree like Uncle Tom did."

"And bring it inside for us so we can decorate it."

Eve had no idea what to say. She decided to take the easy way out and stood to turn on the television set.

"Isn't it time for one of your programs? *Kukla, Fran and Ollie,* maybe?"

Later, after the boys were tucked into bed for the night, Eve tossed the catalogue onto Audrey's lap as she sat watching TV. "What are we going to do about this Wish Book? I'm concerned that the boys still think Christmas is all about Santa Claus and toys."

"I am, too."

"Harry knows from experience that Nana Barrett is willing to buy everything in the book. *And* that she's likely to do it."

Audrey ran her hand through her amber hair. "How do we tell the Barretts that we don't want them to buy so much?"

"I don't know. It won't be an easy conversation to have."

"Can we agree that it has to be done? Before Nana buys out the entire Sears catalogue for them?"

"We'll do it together," Eve replied. "Tomorrow, when we go to their house for brunch after church—before things get even more out of hand than they already are."

Audrey let out her breath with a whoosh. "The Barretts didn't understand when I told them I was going to study nursing. I'm afraid this conversation won't go over very well, either."

"I'm very sorry, now, that I let them spoil Harry and me for four years before you came. The funny thing is, no matter how many things the Barretts gave me, I never really felt satisfied inside. My life still felt like it was missing something. Meanwhile, Harry learned to take all their spoiling for granted."

"I'm also worried about them asking Santa Claus for a father," Audrey said.

Eve winced. She'd been hoping that Audrey wouldn't bring up that uncomfortable issue. "They were just fooling around. They're smart enough to know that people don't buy fathers in the Sears catalogue."

"They're growing up the same way we did. Neither of us had a father who was part of our life."

"We turned out all right, didn't we?" Eve asked, trying to make light of it.

"But I always felt an ache inside. Didn't you?"

"You know very well that I did. But I also had men like George, the gardener, who looked out for me, and Williams, the chauffeur, who taught me how to drive. They helped fill a father's role. Our boys have Granddad Barrett and Grandpa Van and Tom, and now Mr. Hamilton, I suppose."

"Yet they're still asking Santa Claus for a daddy."

"Listen, Audrey. We had this conversation the other day—are you ready to remarry and give Bobby a father?"

"No. Besides, there aren't any for sale in the Wish Book."

"Then let's not talk about it anymore."

Chapter 4

The cook had spread a bountiful Sunday brunch on the Barretts' dining room buffet after church, served in silver chafing dishes, with bone china plates and decorated with an arrangement of red roses and white carnations and holly sprigs. Audrey was reminded of the sumptuous buffet brunches her parents would serve guests at Wellingford Hall. She let Bobby choose whatever he wanted from the selection of pancakes, eggs, sausages, bacon, cinnamon rolls, and fruit, but she carried his plate to the table for him so he wouldn't drop it. The long dining room table seated fourteen people comfortably, but only one end had been set with silver-ware and damask napkins. "So we won't have to shout at each other while we eat," Mrs. Barrett explained.

The food was delicious, as usual, but Audrey was nervous as she silently rehearsed what she and Eve planned to say to Nana about buying too many toys. When everyone had finished eating, the boys begged Nana to follow them into the living room, and Audrey rose quickly to join them, knowing they were about to harangue her with their lists of toys. But Mr. Barrett stopped Audrey, asking, "Do you have a minute, my dear?"

"Yes, of course."

He waited until they were alone. "What's this I hear about you applying for a loan at the bank?" he asked.

For a moment, Audrey couldn't reply. How did he know? Then the light dawned, and she felt a growing fury toward Mr. Hamilton for disclosing her private business. She usually felt a little intimidated by her father-in-law, but today her indignation fueled her courage. "Yes, it's true, I have. The loan will cover my college tuition and other expenses for the nursing program. I plan to take classes full-time next fall."

"Why didn't you ask us for the money, Audrey? You know we're willing to help in any way that we can."

"I know you are. You've been very generous to Bobby and me. But I plan to become a nurse, you see. And I know that you don't quite approve."

"It's not that I disapprove, exactly. It's just that I believe there are other careers that would be more suitable for a woman in your position. Even so, you didn't need to go behind my back."

"I wasn't trying to hide it from you. Honestly, I wasn't. It's just that I want to try to make it on my own. I grew up in a wealthy family, and I took it for granted that I could have anything I wanted. Then during the war, I stood on my own two feet for the first time and learned to make my own way, my own decisions. I felt different about myself after discovering what I was capable of doing on my own." Audrey blinked away the sudden tears that stung her eyes, remembering how she'd been disinherited. The painful truth that she was the result of her mother's adulterous affair still hurt her deeply.

"You're part of our family now. And families help each other out."

"I know they do. And I'm very grateful. But my brother, Alfie, was given everything he wanted, and in the end, wealth became more important to him than

anything else in his life, even love. He became dependent on money and lived a life of leisure, going to par-
ties and drinking too much. He didn't take his studies
at the university seriously."

"I hardly think you're in danger of that, my dear."

She drew a breath, determined to be heard and
understood. "Robert and I talked about how we wanted
to raise our son. Robert wanted to work for a living and
live simply, which is why he built a modest house. And
now I want to teach Bobby how to work for the things
that are important to us."

"But won't you accept the money for your college
tuition as my gift to you?"

His words startled her. She wasn't sure how to
respond. "A-a gift? Thank you, but . . . I want to earn
my own way and pay for my education myself."

"By mortgaging your home?"

"Yes." There seemed nothing more for either of
them to say. "Shall we join the others?" Audrey asked.
The conversation had shaken her, and she wanted to
flee. Yet she and Eve were about to have another difficult conversation with Mrs. Barrett. Why couldn't she
make her in-laws see that Robert hadn't wanted their
money, and neither did she?

"Go ahead," Mr. Barrett said. "I'll be there in a minute."

Audrey made her way to the grand living room, where Nana Barrett was seated on the sofa with Harry and Bobby. The Wish Book was open on her lap. "I don't believe it!" Audrey exclaimed when she saw it.

"I know," Eve said. "Somehow, someway, they found out where we'd hidden it and smuggled it over here."

"We're just having a little look at it together," Nana said. "Where's the harm?"

The catalogue was starting to look wrinkled and dog-eared. "With any luck, it will fall to pieces soon," Eve said.

"I'd like to toss it into the fireplace," Audrey said. She turned away to where a perfect fire was blazing on the hearth, trying to give her temper a chance to cool. Her conversation with Mr. Barrett had upset her—two years of nursing school, as a gift? He didn't understand her at all. And now this business with the Wish Book again.

The Barretts' huge Christmas tree towered in front of the window beside the hearth, and like the rest of the house, it had been beautifully and tastefully decorated, sparkling with hundreds of colored lights.

Some of them, like miniature candles, seemed to be bubbling. Every piece of tinsel had been perfectly positioned on the branches as if placed there one at a time. Perhaps they had been. Beneath the tree, an elaborate train set wound in a figure eight, over bridges and through tunnels, past houses with tiny people and animals.

"Your tree is magnificent," Audrey told Mrs. Barrett.

"The florists always do such a beautiful job, don't they?"

"We got a tree but we didn't put it up, yet," Bobby said. "Mummy says it's too heavy."

"Would you like me to send someone over to help decorate it?"

"Thank you, but I think the boys would enjoy doing it themselves," Audrey said. "They made some decorations for it in kindergarten."

"A big chain out of colored paper," Harry said. "Bobby and I glued ours together to make a really long one."

"And we made stars out of tinfoil in Sunday school today," Bobby added. "Because baby Jesus is a flashlight."

"A flashlight?" Nana asked. Audrey covered her mouth to hide a smile.

"Yep. The teacher turned off the lights and made it really dark," Harry explained. "Then she turned on the flashlight and the dark went away!" He spread his hands as if to say it was magical.

Bobby nodded enthusiastically. "That's what Jesus does. He's like a flashlight in the dark. And He made all the stars. The real ones."

"How lovely," Nana said.

Maybe the boys were finally getting it. But the next moment Harry said, "I want a flashlight for Christmas!"

"Me, too!"

"Did you boys enjoy the Christmas parade?" Nana asked. "Did you sit on Santa's lap and tell him all of the toys you want him to bring?"

"The line was too long. We're writing him letters instead."

"It's taking a *long* time to write, though," Bobby said, "because Mummy will only let us pick one toy from each page."

"And the cowboy boots are on the same page as the cowboy hats!"

"Well, surely boots and hats go together," Nana said. She looked up at Audrey. "Can't you make an exception?"

"We're trying to teach them that Christmas isn't only about Santa Claus and toys," she replied.

"Right. It's about this," Eve said. She gestured to an exquisite porcelain manger scene on display on the living room console. The boys slid off the sofa in unison and made a dash toward it.

Nana gasped. "Careful! Don't touch! Those figurines are very old and quite irreplaceable." Audrey managed to grab the boys and stop them in time.

"But can't I just see the kings, Nana?" Harry asked. "We're gonna be the smart kings in our school play." Audrey lifted him up and pointed to the elaborately painted Wise Men, careful to keep him and Bobby at a safe distance.

"Can you and Granddad come and see our play?" Bobby asked.

"We wouldn't miss it, darling. Let me know when it is."

"It's this Wednesday at their school at seven o'clock," Audrey said.

Mr. Barrett joined them after exchanging his suit jacket for a cardigan sweater. He still wore his tie from church. Audrey wondered if he would show up for the school play in his tuxedo.

The boys ran to him, tugging his hands. "Can you show us the train now, Granddad? Please?"

"My pleasure."

Audrey waited until they'd settled themselves on the floor beneath the tree, the train buzzing and humming on its tracks, then she sat down beside her mother-in-law, steeling herself for another difficult conversation. "Eve and I are concerned that our sons expect to receive everything they want for Christmas. Even if you can afford it, it isn't right. You saw all the toys they're asking for in the Wish Book. Pages and pages of them."

"We want them to know how to work hard and earn money," Eve said. "Please don't indulge all their wishes this Christmas. One gift from you is enough."

Mrs. Barrett's brow puckered. "Well, I already bought them several things, you see." She leaned close to whisper, "Roy Rogers outfits with chaps and vests and cowboy hats and toy pistols with holsters. I didn't buy the boots yet. I wanted to ask you what size they wear."

Audrey sighed. "They both take size five—but then that's all. Please don't buy anything else."

"Well, I thought I might buy them small bicycles with training wheels."

Audrey had a sudden image of the handsome male model from the Sears catalogue running down the street beside Bobby in his suit, holding him steady as he learned to ride without the training wheels. She shook her head to erase it. "Why don't you buy the bikes for their birthdays next summer, instead? That way, they'll be able to ride them right away."

"Well . . . I suppose that makes sense. Oh, I almost forgot. I also bought a darling little portable record player and some records they can share."

"That's plenty. They'll be thrilled."

"But Bobby mentioned just now that they wanted toy fire engines. And sleds. I don't see any harm in—"

Eve leaned forward, covering Mrs. Barrett's hand, stopping her. "Thank you for your generosity. You've always made Christmas so special for the boys. And for me. But Harry and Bobby don't need every toy in the Wish Book in order to be happy. The love you've shown us is more than enough."

Audrey could breathe again. Thank goodness for Eve, who'd managed to sound warm instead of critical. If Audrey had spoken, she knew she would have sounded stiff and cold. She still cringed when she remembered her conversation with Mr. Hamilton at the bank.

"I'm going to order tickets for all of us for the children's Christmas party at the country club," Mrs. Barrett said. "It's on December 20, a Thursday. The boys enjoyed it so much last year—petting the reindeer and meeting Santa Claus." Audrey recalled attending the party last year and remembered that Santa Claus had given a present to every child. Bobby had been sick to his stomach from all the candy and ice cream.

"Please don't buy a ticket for me," Eve said. "I didn't go last year because of the scandal I had caused. And this year I'll be at work all day."

"But Harry can go, can't he?" Nana asked. "And you and Bobby are going with me, aren't you, Audrey?"

Audrey didn't want to go, but she also didn't want to hurt Robert's parents. "Yes, of course I'll go. Thank you."

Audrey left the Barretts' home later that afternoon feeling as though she was a huge disappointment to them as their daughter-in-law. They were offering generous gifts, motivated by love, and they didn't seem to understand why she was refusing them.

After a supper of sausages and beans, Audrey plopped the Wish Book down on the living room coffee table and told the boys, "This is it. It's time to go through the book and make your list. You may choose one toy per page."

"But, Mummy . . ."

"And that doesn't mean that Santa will bring everything on your list," Eve added. "You should let Santa know which two or three toys you want the most."

"Right," Audrey said. "And then the book is going into the rubbish, and that will be the end of it."

Their words brought a chorus of complaints and wails.

"Mummy, no!"

"You can't throw it away!"

"Make up your minds, and when you're ready, we'll write the letters to Santa Claus."

"Can we ask Santa for a dog?" Harry asked. "Dogs aren't in the book."

"We only need one. We can share it."

"No dog until you're much older," Eve said.

"If ever . . . ," Audrey mumbled.

"Please, Mommy?"

"We *need* a dog!"

"Dogs are a lot of work and a lot of responsibility," Eve said. "Bobby's mum will be going to school all day like the two of you, and I'll be at work. It wouldn't be fair to leave a poor dog here all alone."

"I'm still putting it on my list," Harry said stubbornly. "Santa isn't mean like you."

Chapter 5

Audrey was setting the table for dinner when Eve arrived home from work with a big bag from Woolworth's. "I bought this at the dime store on my lunch hour," she said, setting the bag on the counter. She pulled out a large cardboard box with a picture of a manger scene on the outside. "The boys admired the set at the Barretts' house, so I decided we needed one to help them remember why we celebrate Christmas. I got the cheapest one in the store so the boys could touch it and handle it."

"We're thinking alike," Audrey said as she returned to the stove to stir the green beans. "I was remembering what Grandma Van said the other day about Christmas being Jesus' birthday, and I wondered what you would think about having a birthday party on Christmas Day. Maybe even buy a birthday cake."

"Yes! With candles. And Christmas crackers and party hats."

"The boys have been pestering me all afternoon to put up our Christmas tree," Audrey said. "I told them maybe we'd do it tonight."

"I hope the two of us can manage it. That tree is so heavy we may have to tie ropes to it and drag it inside. But then we'll still have to lift it into the stand some-how."

"Should we call Tom? I'm sure he'll be willing to come over and help."

"I don't want to do that." Eve's swift response and the curt way she said it surprised Audrey.

"Why not?"

Eve didn't reply. She slit open the cardboard box and began pulling out plaster figures of sheep and angels, spilling straw packing material on the floor.

"Did you and Tom have a fight or something?" Audrey asked.

"Not exactly. Just a disagreement about . . . timing."

Audrey waited.

"Tom is ready to be more than friends, and I'm not."

"I can tell that he loves you and you love him. What's the problem?"

"I can't explain it. I just need more time." She scooped everything back into the box and left the kitchen.

The moment the boys finished their chocolate pudding after dinner, they started begging to put up the Christmas tree. "Chores first," Audrey said. It was the boys' job to help clear the table, sweep the crumbs from under it—and the straw that Eve had spilled—and empty the rubbish. They were almost finished when the doorbell rang. Audrey went to answer it—and was stunned to see Mr. Hamilton standing on the front step, holding a leather briefcase. "Oh! Hello." Audrey's heart sped up at the sight of him. A banker had no right at all to be so good-looking.

"Hello, Mrs. Barrett. I hope you don't mind me stopping by unannounced, but I thought I would drop off this paperwork so you'd have a chance to read through it before it's time to sign it."

"I-I could have come to the bank."

"Well, I thought I'd save you a trip. I know you're busy." He looked pleased with himself for being helpful, and she was about to thank him—but then Audrey recalled how he'd told Mr. Barrett about the loan and her fury returned. Before she could berate him, Bobby and Harry came running in from the kitchen, grinning and jumping around his legs like puppies.

"We're gonna decorate our Christmas tree," Harry said. "Wanna help?"

Audrey pulled them away. "Will you boys give Mr. Hamilton and me a moment to talk, please? Go help Harry's mum carry the decorations up from the basement." She turned back to Mr. Hamilton as they scampered off. "Come in, please." He removed his hat and followed her into the living room. She needed to remain calm. "I had a very awkward conversation with Mr. Barrett on Sunday. It seems you told him about my loan application before I had a chance to tell him myself. He seemed quite hurt. I tried to explain my reasons, but I'm still not sure he understood."

Mr. Hamilton's smile vanished. "He didn't hear about the loan from me. Maybe my father told him."

"Your father is the bank president. Doesn't he have better things to do with his time than to concern himself with everyday loans like mine?"

Mr. Hamilton winced, clearly embarrassed. "I am

so sorry. Maybe it was my fault that Mr. Barrett found out. You see, I was so impressed by what you told me about standing on your own two feet and setting an example for Bobby—it's so unusual. The young women in my social circle think very differently than you do, and I found your attitude refreshing. And inspiring. I liked what you said about wanting to teach your son the value of earning his way. So I told my father about you. How remarkable you are and how much I admired you. I suppose he mentioned it to your father-in-law at a Rotary meeting or something. I'm really very sorry, Mrs. Barrett. The last thing I wanted to do was cause tension between you and Mr. Barrett. Will you forgive me?" He seemed so sincere that she suddenly felt like the villain in a children's story.

"Yes, of course. I'm sorry for sounding cross. I didn't mean to give you a ticking off."

"Yes, you did." He grinned, revealing that unnerving dimple in his cheek. "And I deserved it. Let me make it up to you."

"You don't have to do that."

"I'll talk to Mr. Barrett myself and tell him how much I admire you and support what you're doing."

"Oh no, please don't do that. You'll only make things

worse. Just leave it alone." She heard footsteps clomping up the basement steps and said, "Now, didn't you say you had some papers for me?"

He had just set his briefcase on the coffee table and snapped it open when Bobby skipped into the room, carrying a cardboard box. "We found the Christmas lights, Mummy! Come on, we have to bring the tree inside!"

Mr. Hamilton handed Audrey a sheaf of papers. "I've taken enough of your time."

Harry marched into the room behind Bobby and set down the box he carried. "Wanna help us, Mr. Hamilton?"

"This is your special family time, Harry. I don't want to intrude."

"Please? *Please?*" they chorused.

Eve entered the living room with a third box, panting from the climb up the basement stairs. "You aren't intruding. The boys are very fond of you, Mr. Hamilton. Besides, I'm not sure Audrey and I can drag the tree inside by ourselves or set it up in the tree stand. We had a hard enough time just pushing it off the roof of the car and shoving it out of the way. We could use your help."

Audrey shot her friend an angry glare. It was unlike Eve to play the helpless maiden. "Mr. Hamilton is wearing an expensive overcoat. He'll get tree sap all over it."

"That's not a problem," he said. "I would be happy to help two damsels in distress." He removed his overcoat and suit jacket and laid them over a chair, then rolled up his shirtsleeves, revealing the fine golden hair on his brawny arms. Audrey looked away, upset with herself for noticing. Eve led him outside, and he came up with the idea of screwing the stand to the tree before carrying it inside to make it easier to set up. He left a trail of pine needles as he lugged it through the door, but he looked quite proud of himself when the tree was finally upright in the stand. The boys cheered.

Before Audrey had a chance to thank him and tell him he could leave, Harry handed him a tangled pile of Christmas lights. "Can you fix these? Mommy can never get them to work."

"They're all different colors when you plug them in," Bobby said. "Like a rainbow."

"But they won't go on."

"They're frustrating, is what they are," Eve said. "If one of them is loose or burned out, the entire string goes off, so you can't tell which one is the culprit. It might even be more than one."

"I'll see if I can help." Mr. Hamilton sat down on the edge of the sofa and began untangling the string while Eve and the boys dug through the boxes of decorations, pulling out ornaments.

"Let me give you a hand," Audrey said, hoping to be rid of him sooner. Together they untangled the long string, and Mr. Hamilton began the painstaking task of testing and twisting and shaking one bulb after the other to get the string to light. Audrey actually saw a bead of sweat on his brow. "Have you ever done this before, Mr. Hamilton?"

"I wish you would call me Alan."

"You didn't answer my question . . . Alan."

"No, I can't say that I ever have."

"Didn't you have a Christmas tree when you were a little boy?" Bobby asked.

"Yes, of course. But someone else always decorated it for our family." He screwed another light into the socket and suddenly they all lit up. "Success at last!" He beamed as brightly as the lights. He took one end of the string and Audrey took the other and they wound the lights around the tree.

"You can reach up real high, Mr. Hamilton," Harry said.

"Will you put this star on top for us, too?" Bobby asked.

"How about if I lift you up so you can put it on top?" He swung Bobby off the floor and lifted him up to put the star in place. Then he lowered him again and stood back to look. "I guess my work here is finished."

"Yes, thanks again—" Audrey began.

But Eve cut her off. "Oh, but you can't quit now. We still have all these decorations to hang and the tinsel and the paper chains the boys made in school."

"Don't forget our tinfoil stars."

"You made this?" Mr. Hamilton asked, admiring the star Bobby showed him. "Very nice."

Eve put a Bing Crosby Christmas album on the phonograph, and Audrey relaxed enough to sing along with "White Christmas" and other favorites while they worked. By the time they hung the tinsel, which seemed to be electrically charged and clung to their hair and clothing, Audrey was laughing along with everyone else. The finished tree was nothing like Nana Barrett's perfect one, but she thought theirs was beautiful, just the same.

"Mr. Hamilton?" Bobby asked. "Can you cut off some branches on the bottom for us?"

"Why? It looks very nice the way it is."

"Santa is going to need more room under it for toys."

"Santa will have all of the room he needs," Audrey said, steering Bobby away. "I think Mr. Hamilton wants to go home now."

"Do you really have to go?" Eve asked. "I just made tea." She set the tray with the pot and cups on the coffee table. "And we're going to set up our new manger scene now and read the Christmas story from the Bible."

Audrey rolled her eyes. "Eve . . ."

"I telephoned Grandma Van and she helped me find all the places to read from in the New Testament."

"We're in a Christmas play at school," Harry said. "Will you come and see us, Mr. Hamilton?"

Bobby tugged his hand. "Please?"

"Tell me when and where, and I'll see if I'm free."

"Please don't feel obligated, Mr. Ham—I mean, Alan," Audrey said.

"Not at all. There will probably be several kids from my Boys' Club group taking part in it."

Audrey set the wooden stable on top of the TV console and helped the boys divide up all the plaster figurines between them. There was one Wise Man left over, so they gave it to Mr. Hamilton. Then, as they sipped tea and Eve read the Bible story, Harry and Bobby took turns putting shepherds and sheep and angels and the holy family into their places in the stable whenever Eve read that part of the story. Mr. Hamilton wore a contented look as his Wise Man went into place last.

"Remember what Grandma Van said?" Audrey asked the boys. "Jesus is God's gift to us." They didn't seem to hear her as they disappeared into their bedroom. They came out a few minutes later with their hands full of plastic cowboys and horses, Howdy Doody and Clarabell, the Lone Ranger and Tonto. Even Mr. Potato Head.

"What are you going to do with all of those?" Audrey asked.

"They want to see baby Jesus, too," Bobby said.

She watched in amusement as the top of the television console was gradually covered with visitors.

"I have a confession to make," Alan Hamilton said as he carried the tea tray into the kitchen. "I didn't need to bring the papers over tonight, but I wanted to see you. And I'm glad I did. I had fun tonight. Christmas wasn't like this in my family when I was growing up."

"Mine, neither." Her earlier opinion of him had softened, and she was glad, for the boys' sakes, that he had stayed. "Do you have brothers and sisters, Alan?"

"Three sisters. I was the youngest child and the only boy. That's why I was so desperate to escape to Boys' Club when I was young."

Audrey laughed as she took the tray from him and set it on the counter. "Thank you for helping us with the tree."

"There's another reason I came tonight. I'd like to ask you to go to a Christmas dinner with me. The bank holds it every year for their employees. It's at the country club, but it's not a formal event or anything. Just dinner and dancing. I would like it very much if you'd be my date."

Audrey's heart started thumping. "Is that allowed . . . to date a client?"

"Well, I would rather think of you as a friend than a client."

"I-I don't know."

"I know it isn't fair to spring the question on you so suddenly, but please think about it. You can let me know when I see you at the school play."

Eve looked very pleased with herself after Alan left,

but Audrey was still annoyed with her. "Why did you keep encouraging him to stay? I didn't think he would ever go home."

"The boys adore him."

"And you kept insisting we needed his help."

"Are you really that blind, Audrey? Alan likes you."

"Don't be absurd."

"I heard him invite you to dinner."

"You were eavesdropping?"

"It's a small house," she said with a shrug. "Why didn't you say yes?"

"I don't want to go to a Christmas party with him and his rich friends at the country club. We have nothing in common."

Eve laughed out loud. "Nothing in common! What are you talking about? Now, if Alan Hamilton had asked *me* out, I could honestly say we had nothing in common, considering that I was once a scullery maid. I had to put on an award-winning act every time I went to the country club and tried to fit in with the other women. But you, my dear, were born into that life. Your family was just as rich as Alan Hamilton's. You not only socialized with royalty, but your father probably had more money than King George."

"He wasn't my father," Audrey murmured. It still hurt to remember. "Alfred Clarkson wasn't my father."

Eve saw Audrey's tears and pulled her into her arms. "I'm sorry, Audrey. I wasn't thinking."

"I don't know why I feel so weepy," she said when Eve released her again and she'd brushed away her tears. "Christmas is supposed to be a happy time, but I keep thinking that Robert should be the one who lifts Bobby onto his shoulders to see the parade. Robert should be helping me put up the Christmas tree and boosting Bobby up to put the star on top."

"Remembering will probably always be hard," Eve said. "But Robert wouldn't want you to mourn forever."

"I know. I know. But I'm not sure he'd be happy to see me drinking tea with the banker's wealthy son."

"Why not? You know, when you describe Alan's family as rich and entitled, aren't you also describing Robert and his family?"

"Yes, but that's not the way Robert and I wanted to live."

"Don't you think you're being a bit too judgmental to reject a nice bloke like Alan Hamilton simply because he's rich and comes from a good family? He's a very nice guy, Audrey. I couldn't find a single fault with him tonight—he even managed to get the light strings to work. He's a Boys' Club leader, for goodness' sake. How many snooty country-club men do you know who would volunteer to lead a group of kindergarten boys? How many other gentlemen would wrestle with someone else's Christmas tree in his starched shirt and pin-striped trousers?"

"I hope the tree sap didn't ruin his clothes."

"And he is very attractive—or didn't you notice?" She began poking Audrey in the shoulder until she squirmed away, grinning.

"I guess I did notice."

"He has dimples."

"Only one. In his left cheek." Audrey had wanted to touch it.

"Hooray! You did notice! Go with him, Audrey. Get to know him a little better before you decide whether or not he's your type. It's just dinner. What's the harm? You might even have fun." Eve paused, then asked, "What are you so afraid of?"

Audrey closed her eyes, remembering. "When I lost Robert, I wanted to die. I don't ever want to feel that much pain again."

"Then you'll have to stop living, because life is going

to bring pain. It's a certainty. I loved Alfie. I didn't think I could ever love anyone that much. But I loved Harry's father too, and that pain is still with me because he wasn't mine to love. To this day, the shame I feel makes the pain even worse."

"Are you afraid to love Tom?"

"Maybe. But we aren't talking about me, Audrey; we're talking about you. Did you see Alan's face tonight when he was helping us? He was enjoying himself, in spite of being all thumbs."

Audrey smiled, picturing his grin when the lights finally went on. "He told me he'd never decorated a Christmas tree before. And he thanked me for letting him help."

"Maybe he doesn't buy into the wealthy lifestyle, either. Maybe he wants what you have. Promise me you'll give him a chance. Promise me you'll accept his dinner invitation."

Audrey sighed, then nodded. "All right. But I must be crazy."

Chapter 6

13 DAYS BEFORE CHRISTMAS

Eve's workday had been a busy one, and she felt as though she'd barely had a chance to eat supper and catch her breath before it was time to leave for the Christmas program at school. She was in the boys' bedroom, trying to tame Harry's springy red hair with a wet comb, when he asked, "Can we have the Wish Book back again? Bobby and I need to change something."

"We already mailed your letters to Santa Claus, remember?"

"I know, but we need to tell Santa we changed our mind."

"What did you change your mind about?" Audrey asked. She was trying to prod Bobby off his bunk and into his trousers and shoes.

"Well, if there's *two* things we want on the same page," Harry said, "Santa can give one to Bobby and one to me—and then we can share."

"It's very nice that you've decided to share," Eve said. "I'm happy to hear it."

"So can we have the book?"

"Maybe later. Let's go or we're going to be late."

"That was sweet of the boys to decide to share, wasn't it?" Audrey asked after she and Eve had taken their seats in the school cafeteria for the play. The lunch tables had been folded and stacked to the side, and rows of chairs faced a makeshift stage. The sound of children's voices echoed in the large room, threatening Eve with a headache.

"I'm very suspicious of their new plan," she told Audrey. "I think it might be just a clever ploy to get more toys. And I foresee more than a few squabbles when the time comes to share."

"You're being very cynical."

"I'm being realistic—and do you really want to see the Wish Book make a reappearance in your house?"

They had saved seats for the boys' guests—Grandma and Grandpa Van and Tom, who sat beside Eve, and Mr. and Mrs. Barrett, who sat beside Audrey. Eve was glancing around as the school cafeteria filled with parents and grandparents. She spotted Alan Hamilton standing in the back.

"He came," she said, nudging Audrey. "Alan Hamilton is here. Go back and invite him to sit with us."

"That seems a bit nervy."

"He's here to see Bobby and Harry. They invited him, remember? And don't forget, you promised me you would accept his dinner invitation tonight." Audrey sighed and went back to speak with him. "Move over so there will be an empty seat for him beside Audrey," Eve whispered to Tom.

Alan greeted the Barretts, who seemed surprised to see him. "The boys invited Alan," Audrey was quick to say. "He's their Boys' Club leader at church." Eve made all of the other introductions, and Alan and Tom remembered each other from high school. "We played football together," Alan explained.

"That was a long time ago, wasn't it?" Tom said, chuckling.

The lights dimmed and the program began with

children from the upper grades reciting poems like "'Twas the night before Christmas," singing carols, and playing a few ear-piercing numbers on their song flutes. Finally it was time for the kindergarten class to present their play about the Christmas story.

"I'm nervous for Bobby," Audrey whispered. "He's usually so shy."

The boys' teacher, Miss Powell, led most of the kindergarten children, dressed in Christmas finery, onto one side of the stage to form a choir. Mary and Joseph shuffled onto the other side of the stage, trying not to trip over their long robes. They approached the innkeeper, who stood with his arms folded across his chest, looking grumpy. "We need a room for the night," Joseph said.

"There's *no room in the inn*!" he shouted. "It's *full*!" Mary backed up a step, clearly upset by his words or perhaps by the way he had bellowed them at her. When she seemed about to burst into tears, the innkeeper had a change of heart. "Wait. Would you like to come in and have a drink of water?"

"I don't remember that part in the Bible," Tom whispered as the audience chuckled. Mary might have accepted his offer, but Miss Powell was waving vigorously from the other side of the stage, shaking her head and motioning for the holy couple to sit down inside the stable in the center of the stage. An angel with filmy wings, a white robe, and a lopsided halo waited there for them.

The angel drew a breath as if about to go deep-sea diving and said in a rush, "That-night-baby-Jesus-was-borned." Mary reached behind the bale of straw she was sitting on and produced a towel-wrapped doll. She held the doll close, rocking it in her arms as Miss Powell cued the rest of the kindergarten children to sing.

"'Away in a manger, no crib for a bed . . .'"

But the baby wasn't in the manger; he was still in Mary's arms. The angel tried to snatch him away. "Baby Jesus is *supposed* to go in the *manger!*" she hissed.

"No! I'm holding him!" A tug-of-war broke out between the two that yanked the doll's arm from its socket and required Joseph to mediate.

"'But little Lord Jesus no crying He makes,'" the children sang.

"And keep him there!" Joseph said as he plunked the doll and its severed arm into the manger. Mary burst into tears. She tried to run from the stage, but Miss Powell caught her and coaxed her back to her hay bale in the stable. She also herded three choir members back to their places after they'd wandered over to see baby Jesus' mangled arm.

Eve glanced at Audrey and covered her mouth to keep from laughing.

It was time for the shepherds. The teacher nodded to someone on the opposite side of the stage, and a band of shepherds wandered out in their bathrobes, trying not to trip over their "sheep"—children covered in cotton wadding and walking on their hands and knees. While the choir sang another out-of-tune verse about the shepherds, several sheep began to wander. The shepherds tried to corral them with their staffs, and it turned into a free-for-all with shepherds prodding sheep and sheep trying to grab the staffs from their hands.

Mercifully, the song ended and a young angel, who obviously aspired to be a ballerina, pirouetted onto the stage. After two dizzying twirls that brought her perilously close to the edge of the stage, she made her announcement: "Fear not! A Savior has been born to you . . . so *stop fighting*!" Her shouts ended the wrestling match between shepherds and sheep. "You will find the baby in wadded-up clothes and lying in a . . . um . . ."

"Manger!" Joseph shouted.

"Oh yeah, a manger." She started to twirl and pirouette her way off stage, then stopped and said, "He's in Bethlehem! I was supposed to say in Bethlehem!"

"Did they actually rehearse this?" Tom whispered with a grin. Eve poked him with her elbow.

One of the shepherds took a step forward and said, "Let's go and see this . . . this . . . Let's go and see this crazy thing . . . that . . . that just happened." His sigh of relief after delivering his line could be heard in the back row. The shepherds and their flock ambled across the stage to the manger, the sheep bleating loudly as if trying to outdo each other, while the choir mumbled their way through a verse about angels.

"Be *quiet!*" Mary shouted above it all. "Baby Jesus is trying to sleep!" She reached into the manger to cover the doll's ears.

With the shepherds and sheep successfully shuffled to the side, it was time for the Wise Men to arrive. "Here we go," Eve whispered. Three little kings with tinfoil crowns marched out in a line while the choir sang. Another boy was leading, then Harry, then Bobby, who stared down at the floor, his face pale, as if he was either on his way to a funeral or about to throw up.

"Oh no. I think he has stage fright," Audrey whispered.

"I hope Miss Powell has a mop handy," Eve replied.

The first king gazed straight ahead as he strode majestically toward the manger to deliver his gift. Harry was more interested in the audience than he was in Jesus, and he peered out at the crowd, grinning from ear to ear as he scanned all the faces. When he saw Eve and the rest of his family, his face lit up and he began to wave. Eve scrunched lower in her seat. Harry turned around and nudged Bobby, pointing to their family as if urging him to wave, too. Bobby shook his head, still staring at the floor.

They were almost to the manger when Harry, who wasn't watching where he was going, bumped into the first Wise Man. The boy turned and gave Harry a shove, which made him stumble backwards into Bobby. Naturally, Harry shoved the boy back.

Miss Powell scurried over to separate the two, saying, "Give the baby your gifts. Please!" She was clearly eager to be done with this play.

The first Wise Man laid his box beside the manger. Harry stepped up next and said, "Mine is full of gold, see?" He opened it, tipping it a little too far, and a cascade of foil-wrapped chocolate coins spilled out, rolling across the stage.

"Candy!" one of the sheep said, and the flock scampered forward on all fours to scoop it up. "Hey! That candy is for Jesus!" Harry shouted. "Give it back!" Once again, the exasperated teacher had to restore order as the audience roared with laughter.

"Well, I'll be moving back to England now," Eve said.

"No, this is hysterical," Tom said. "I'm so glad I didn't miss this."

When the laughter died away, it was Bobby's turn to present his gift. "I brought you this," he said, setting down his box. "And this." He lifted his kingly robe and dug in his pant pocket, producing a small stuffed rabbit, which he set on top of the injured doll. The audience gave a collective sigh. "Awww."

"Bobby saves the day!" Tom whispered. Eve gave him another poke. The melee finally ended with the entire kindergarten class singing "We Wish You a Merry Christmas."

Nana Barrett was beaming as she applauded. "That was wonderful! Wonderful!"

Her husband frowned. "Were we watching the same performance?"

Eve looked at Audrey and they burst out laughing.

There were cookies for the children afterwards and coffee for the grown-ups. Harry bounded over to Tom, asking, "Did you see me? Did you see me?"

"Couldn't miss you, kiddo. You did great." He picked Harry up and swung him through the air before setting him down again. Grandma Van pulled him into her arms for a hug. Tears filled Eve's eyes. They looked just like all of the other happy families with mommies and daddies and grandparents—but they weren't a family. Maybe they never would be. She stepped back to distance herself from Tom and his parents.

"Thank you all for coming," she said. "You really didn't have to." Her tone came out colder than she'd intended.

Tom gave her a hard look. "You don't need to thank us, Eve. My parents and I are family, aren't we? Of course, we would come."

Eve turned away and tried to soften the impression she'd just made by thanking the Barretts and Alan Hamilton for coming, as well. When she turned to speak with Tom again, he had disappeared.

* * *

Audrey told Harry and Bobby to change into their pajamas when they got home, "But you may stay up a bit later tonight since there's no school tomorrow." Of course, Eve would still have to go to work tomorrow and couldn't be with her son. She plugged in the Christmas tree lights and sank down on the sofa, still upset that Tom hadn't said goodbye.

"Listen, Eve," Audrey said, turning to her. "You know how we've been talking about trying to curb the boys' long wish list this Christmas? And how we want to teach them what Christmas is really about? Well, I've been thinking about it for days now, and along with the birthday party for Jesus, what if we also—?"

"Wait. Did you accept Alan's dinner invitation tonight?" she asked Audrey.

"I did."

"Good. Now you can continue."

Audrey was about to say more, but the boys thundered into the living room in their pajamas, carrying a platoon of tin soldiers and Bobby's stuffed bunny. They added them to the manger scene on the TV console.

"I'll tell all of you at the same time," Audrey said when they finished arranging the toys. "I had an idea while I was watching your inspiring performance—"

"Our *what*?"

"Your play . . . when I was watching your play. The Wise Men gave gifts to Jesus, right?"

"Mine was gold!" Harry said.

"Yes. Well, since Christmas is about giving gifts and not just receiving them, I think we should give away some gifts, too. To help people somehow. Just like the Wise Men did."

"That's a wonderful idea, Audrey!"

"You boys have money in your piggy banks that you can use to buy the presents—"

"But that's *my* money," Harry whined. "I worked for it, doing chores."

"Where do you think the money comes from to buy our food or pay for our clothes?" Eve asked. "Somebody has to work for it."

"If you don't want to spend the money in your piggy bank," Audrey said, "you can do extra chores and earn more."

Harry sagged to the floor, sighing dramatically. "*More* work?"

"I don't want to open my piggy bank," Bobby said.

"Well . . ." Audrey raked her fingers through her hair, her frustration clear. "Why don't we start by going through your toy box tomorrow and picking out some toys that you can give away to children who don't have as many as you do?"

The boys looked horrified. "*Our* toys?" Bobby asked.

Harry groaned. "This keeps getting worse and worse!"

"You have so many toys there's hardly room for any more on your shelves."

"Can't we get new shelves?" Bobby asked.

"Bobby, some children have no toys at all."

"Can't Santa bring them some?"

"I think your mummy's idea is an excellent one," Eve said, clapping her hands. "When I was your age, I was one of the children who didn't have very many things. Your mum was very kind to me, and she used to share her books with me because I didn't have any books at all at my house."

"It's wonderful to share what you have," Audrey said. "We want you boys to see for yourselves how nice it is. We can be just like the real Wise Men, giving away gifts."

"And I think I know who the first gift should go to," Eve said. "Remember that little run-down house we pass on the way to Grandma Van's farm? I've seen children playing outside, and I think they would enjoy getting some toys for Christmas."

"Wonderful!" Audrey said. "I'll call Grandma Van tomorrow and see if she knows anything about them."

But when Eve looked down at the mutinous looks on the boys' faces, she didn't see much hope of Audrey's plan succeeding.

Chapter 7

"Yay! No more school," Bobby cheered as he gulped his Rice Krispies the next morning.

"Let's build a snow fort! Want to?" Harry had finished his cereal, and he lifted his bowl to drink the last of his milk from it, then he wiped his mouth with the back of his hand. Bobby lifted his bowl to imitate Harry, but Audrey stopped him in time.

"Use a spoon, please. We don't slurp from our cereal bowls. You both know better." Yet she wondered if she was being too proper. Would Eve say they were just being boys? They carried their bowls and juice glasses to the sink, then raced to the coat hooks to put on their galoshes and jackets and snow pants. "Wait," Audrey said. "Remember what we talked about last night? About being like the Wise Men and giving away gifts for Jesus' birthday?"

"We don't want to be Wise Men anymore," Harry said. Bobby nodded in agreement.

"Well, Harry's mum and I decided that giving gifts is going to be our new Christmas tradition. You may go outside and build your snow fort in a little while," she said, taking the coats from their hands. "But first, I want you to look through your toy box and pick out some toys to give away to children who don't have any." She gently directed them toward their bedroom.

"But, Mummy, I like all of my toys."

"What if we can't find any to give away?" Harry asked.

"Maybe Santa Claus will decide you don't need any new toys if your shelves and toy box are already full."

"But . . . that's not fair!"

"Would you like me to help you pick out some?" she asked when they reached their room. "I can make a few suggestions."

"We can do it," Harry said with a sigh.

"Good. I'll check back with you after I wash the breakfast dishes." Audrey telephoned Grandma Van after tidying the kitchen and told her about their gift-giving plan. "Eve and I wondered if the family who lives down the road from your farm could use some things for Christmas? They don't seem to have very much."

"I think that's a wonderful idea," Grandma Van said. "The Robertsons have three little boys, none of them in school yet. I bring eggs and milk to them from time to time. Maybe Tom can chop down a Christmas tree for them, too. And do you think Harry and Bobby would like to come over and help me bake cookies for them?"

"I'm sure they would."

"Come over anytime this afternoon and we'll start baking."

Audrey was discouraged to see that Bobby and Harry had chosen only six toys to give away, all in need of repair. "The Robertson boys are younger than you, so let's find some toys that you've outgrown." Audrey knelt beside the toy box and began digging through it. "What about these blocks? And this wooden boat? You don't play with this game anymore, do you?" She pulled out several more toddler items, then stood to scan the shelves. "You don't read these picture books anymore.

And here's a ball. You have several other balls." She looked around the room. "What about this wooden rocking horse?"

"I like that horse, Mummy."

"I know, but you're getting too big for it. You seldom play with it. Why not let someone else enjoy it?" She helped them choose a few more toys that were better suited to younger children, then combed through their drawers and closet for clothes and shoes and boots that they had outgrown.

With their pile of toys complete, Audrey set the boys free to build their snow fort until lunchtime.

*   *   *

Later that afternoon, they drove out to the farm together to bake cookies. Audrey slowed the car as they passed the run-down house where the Robertson family lived. "Do you see those little boys playing in the snow?" she asked. "They're the ones you're giving your toys to, for your first Wise Man gift. It looks like they don't have very many toys, doesn't it?"

"The house looks like it's falling over," Harry said.

"Do they have food?" Bobby asked.

"Not as much as we have, I'm sure. That's why Grandma Van is going to help you bake cookies for them. And I brought along the toys you picked out so you can ask Grandpa Van and Uncle Tom to help you repair them."

Tom and his father were happy to help when they saw the toys. "These shouldn't be too hard to fix," Grandpa said after looking them over.

"I have some extra paint we can use to spruce them up a bit, too," Tom said.

"If it isn't too much trouble," Audrey said, "I would be grateful if you helped the boys do some of the work themselves so they'll learn how. Eve and I are trying to teach them that it's fun to give away gifts. It's a surprise they haven't discovered yet, and they could use a good lesson in giving."

"Sure thing. I'll gather the tools we'll need and we can get to work on these toys once the cookies are in the oven."

Audrey felt happy and content for the first time in a long time as she sat in the cheerful, farmhouse kitchen helping the boys and Grandma Van mix flour and butter and sugar to make Christmas cookies. Grandma showed them how to roll out the dough, and she let the boys cut them into Christmas shapes with cookie cutters. Flour dusted their faces and the fronts of their sweater vests. Audrey couldn't recall ever experiencing an afternoon like this one, certainly not during her own childhood, but she was grateful that her son had the chance to be here. There was so much love in this home, and it baffled Audrey that Eve would turn away from becoming part of it. Tom loved Eve, and she loved him. Audrey didn't understand it, and Eve refused to explain it.

"We'll put icing and sprinkles on the cookies after they've cooled," Grandma said. "Let's wash your hands and you can head downstairs to the toy workshop in the basement."

Audrey helped Tom's mother mix up a few more batches of different kinds of cookies to go into the freezer until later, while the boys worked with Grandpa and Tom in the basement. She could hear their voices and giggles coming up the stairwell and knew they were probably peppering Tom with their endless questions. She heard his deep voice as he patiently replied. They came upstairs an hour later, their hands and faces speckled with paint. "A little turpentine will clean them right up," Grandpa said with a wink. The odor filled the kitchen as he dabbed at the paint spots with a dampened cloth. "There. Wash up with soap and water and you'll be good as new."

"The children are going to like their toys now," Bobby announced.

"Yeah! They're all fixed up again."

The boys spent another hour smearing colored icing on the cookies and slathering them with sprinkles until it was time to go home.

"We'll come back with Harry's mum on Saturday," Audrey promised, "so we can cut down a Christmas tree for them and deliver our gifts."

"The paint will be all dry by then," Tom said.

The boys pressed their noses to the car window as they drove past the Robertsons' house again on the way home. "Do they have decorations for their tree, Mummy?" Bobby asked.

"I'm not really sure."

"We could make some," Harry said.

"But they'll need lights. We can't make lights." Bobby was quiet for a moment, then said, "Could we stop at the store and buy lights, Mummy?"

"We could . . ."

"But stop at home first," Harry said, "so we can get money from our piggy banks."

* * *

Audrey blinked back tears as she watched Bobby and Harry pry open the bottoms of their piggy banks and shake out the coins. She wished Eve were here to witness their eager generosity.

They drove into town to the Woolworth store, and Audrey helped the boys pick out a package of plastic ornaments, a string of colored lights, and a box of tinsel. She also added a tree stand and two rolls of Christmas wrapping paper to their order. The boys stood on tiptoes to empty the contents of their pockets onto the counter by the cash register.

"Mummy?" Bobby asked. "Is there enough to buy them a new toy, too?"

"What did you have in mind?" They hurried back to the toy section and searched through the items on display, deciding on three mesh Christmas stockings for seventy-nine cents apiece that contained an assortment of plastic toys for little boys. Audrey was surprised and pleased that the boys didn't ask for any new toys for themselves.

The afternoon light was fading when they stepped outside with their purchases, and it was starting to snow again. Audrey looked at her watch. "You know, Harry, if we wait a few more minutes, your mum's bus should be arriving. We can give her a ride home."

Eve's weary expression changed to delight when she stepped off the bus and saw them waiting for her.

Harry hurled himself into her arms. "You know what, Mommy? We baked cookies with Grandma Van and fixed up our old toys and bought decorations and Christmas stockings for the poor children."

"They spent their own money, too," Audrey added.

"It sounds like you've had a fun day."

"We like being smart kings and bringing presents."

They started walking back to where Audrey had parked her car and were almost to the bank when Alan Hamilton came out of the door. Harry ran up to him and grabbed one of his hands. "Mr. Hamilton! Guess what?" He began a long-winded explanation about the Wise Men and the three gifts and the cookies and the toys and the Christmas tree and the stockings from Woolworth's. He paused only long enough to take a breath and for Bobby, who had grabbed his other hand to add, "Me, too! Me, too!"

"We're going to take everything to their house on Saturday," Harry finally finished, "and give them all their presents."

"You're welcome to join us, Alan—" Eve began.

But Audrey was quick to interrupt. "I'm sure Mr. Hamilton is a very busy man." Why was Eve being so pushy with him?

"You know," Alan said, "the bank gives out food baskets to needy families every Christmas. I would be happy to make sure this family gets one of them. When are you doing this?"

"On Saturday, so Eve can come with us," Audrey said.

"Please come, Mr. Hamilton," Bobby said. "You can help us carry the tree inside like you did before."

"If you come to our house first," Eve said, "we could drive out there together. But make sure to wear boots. We'll be tramping through the snow out at Tom's farm to cut down the Christmas tree."

"Please don't feel obligated—" Audrey began.

But Alan flashed his dimpled smile. "Actually, I think I am free on Saturday afternoon. I would love to join you."

Chapter 8

Eve hadn't seen Mrs. Herder and her dog for the past few mornings or evenings as she'd walked to and from work, and it worried her. Her concern deepened as she passed the older woman's house on Friday afternoon and saw two inches of fresh snow on her sidewalk that hadn't been shoveled. Had she gone away for the holiday? Eve paused in front and heard the faint sound of barking coming from inside. The dog stood at the front window. Eve turned up the walkway and onto the porch and rang the doorbell. The barking grew louder and more frantic. At last, the curtain parted on one of the sidelights beside the front door and Mrs. Herder peered out, frowning. The carved oak door opened a crack.

"Yes?"

"Hello, Mrs. Herder? I'm your neighbor, Eve Dawson. I live in one of the new bungalows down the street."

"Yes, I recognize you. Come in, it's too cold to stand here with the door open." The dog circled and pranced around Eve, its toenails clacking on the hardwood floor like typewriter keys.

Eve reached to pet him. "Hey, doggy. How are you?"

"Cooper! Go lie down!" Mrs. Herder said. The Labrador looked up at his owner, tail wagging, but made no attempt to obey.

"I don't mind," Eve said, scratching behind his ears. "I like dogs. Listen, I came because I haven't seen you walking with him for the past couple of days, and when I saw that your sidewalk hadn't been cleared, I was concerned."

"You don't even know me."

Eve turned her attention away from the dog and looked at her neighbor. "Oh! You've injured your ankle!"

Mrs. Herder held a cane in her hand, and her ankle was wrapped in a thick bandage. So was her wrist. "I slipped on the ice. Twisted my ankle and then hurt my wrist when I tried to catch myself."

"Do you need to see a doctor? I can drive you there. I drove an ambulance during the war—"

"The doctor has already come. He told me to stay off my feet—which I'm obviously not doing at the moment."

"Can I get you anything? Do you need groceries?"

"The store makes deliveries, Mrs. . . . Sorry, I didn't catch your name."

"Eve Dawson. I live on the next block with my son, Harry, my friend Audrey, and her son, Bobby."

"Is yours the redhead or the dark-haired one? I've seen them playing outside."

"Mine is the redhead."

"You're British?"

"Yes. Audrey and I met the boys' fathers during the war when they were stationed in England before D-Day, and—"

Mrs. Herder looked away. "I shouldn't be standing on this ankle. It was kind of you to stop by, seeing as we're strangers." She reached down to grip the dog's collar and hold him back, making it clear to Eve that she was dismissed.

Eve felt like kicking herself all the way home for

mentioning the war. Why hadn't she remembered the gold star in Mrs. Herder's window? And yet the visit had given her a great idea for the boys' second Wise Man gift.

"You know the little gray-haired woman who goes by here all the time with her big Labrador?" she asked Audrey the moment she stepped into the kitchen. "She lives in that nice old house on the corner?"

"The one with the gold star in the window?"

"Yes. Well, she fell and twisted her ankle and hurt her wrist. What if the boys helped her by shoveling her sidewalk tomorrow morning for their second gift? And maybe we can offer to walk her dog for her."

"A dog, Mommy?" Harry asked, running into the kitchen. "Are we getting a dog?"

"No, I was talking about Mrs. Herder's dog. You've seen that big yellow dog that goes by here every day with his owner."

"Is it a nice dog?" Bobby asked. He looked a little frightened.

"He's very friendly. You'll have fun with him. His name is Cooper."

"We can bring her some of the cookies we baked with Grandma Van," Bobby said.

"That's a wonderful idea."

*   *   *

They rang Mrs. Herder's doorbell the next morning after breakfast. "Hi, I'm back," Eve said after Mrs. Herder had hobbled to the door. Eve bent to pet Cooper so he would stop barking. "My friend Audrey and I and our two boys have come to clear your sidewalk for you, if that's okay."

"That's very kind, but—"

"We're like the three smart kings," Harry said, pushing up beside her. "I mean, the wise kings . . . no, the Wise *Men*. We're giving presents to people."

"We brought cookies for you, too," Bobby said. He handed her the wrapped plate.

"The chocolate ones are the best," Harry added.

"So if it's okay with you, Mrs. Herder, we'll get busy out here," Eve said. "And when we're done, we would love it if you would let us walk Cooper for you. I'm sure he's tired of being stuck inside."

"I don't know what to say." Mrs. Herder smiled faintly. "Thank you."

"You're very welcome. Well, we'll get busy now. Don't stand on that ankle too long."

"Cooper will be a very grateful dog."

The snow was only a few inches deep, so Eve and Audrey stood back and let the boys do as much of the shoveling as they could manage by themselves, using the snow shovel they'd brought from home and the one propped on Mrs. Herder's porch.

"This is fun!" Bobby announced as they scraped their shovels on the cement and flung snow in every direction.

"We're big and strong, aren't we, Mommy?" Harry held up his arm to show his muscles, invisible beneath his winter coat. Clumps of snow stuck to the boys' mittens and fell inside their galoshes as they worked. Their socks were going to be soaked.

When they were done, Eve and Audrey tidied up their work a bit, making sure the public sidewalk and the walkway to Mrs. Herder's house were thoroughly cleared, while the boys made snow angels on the front lawn. Eve saw Mrs. Herder sitting on a chair by the front window with Cooper beside her, watching them.

"Shall we take Mrs. Herder's dog out now?" Eve asked when they finished. Bobby seemed a little afraid at first but quickly made friends with Cooper once Harry did. They took turns holding his leash as they walked around the block with him.

"Make sure you hold on tightly," Audrey said. "Cooper seems to have a lot of energy."

"Why does he keep stopping and smelling everything?" Harry asked.

"That's what dogs do," Eve replied with a shrug. "It's their way of exploring." The boys played fetch with Cooper in Mrs. Herder's backyard afterwards, tossing the ball to him again and again. Mrs. Herder had made coffee, and Eve and Audrey sat at the kitchen table with her, watching the boys play with their new friend. Cooper was a tease, pretending to offer them the slimy ball, then refusing to relinquish it, playing tug-of-war whenever Harry or Bobby tried to grab it. The sound of their giggles as they rolled in the snow with the dog made even Mrs. Herder smile. When the boys and the dog were tired out, Mrs. Herder insisted they come inside and warm up before walking home.

"Let me pay you for shoveling the sidewalk—" she began.

"No, please, this is our gift to you. The boys were Wise Men in their school play, you see, and like the first Wise Men, we've decided to give gifts to people this Christmas."

"And we want to come every day and walk Cooper for you until your ankle is better," Audrey added.

"At least let me pay you for that."

"Not a chance. The boys enjoyed themselves."

"How come you don't have a Christmas tree?" Harry asked when they went into Mrs. Herder's living room.

"It's too much bother to put one up this year, especially with my lame ankle and wrist."

Eve wondered if they should offer to help her, then decided not to overwhelm her all at once. The furnishings in Mrs. Herder's elegant, old house reminded Eve of Audrey's family's London town house, with Victorian bric-a-brac and a horsehair sofa and Turkish carpets on the polished oak floors.

Eve spotted a picture of a young man in uniform on the fireplace mantel and wondered if she should say something. Mrs. Herder had seemed to shut down the last time she was here and had mentioned the war. But Eve also knew that remaining silent about lost loved ones was sometimes worse—as if they'd never existed. She decided to take a chance. "Is this your son?" she asked, holding her breath.

Mrs. Herder didn't look at the picture, gazing instead at Harry and Bobby, who were sitting on the floor, petting Cooper. "Yes, that's Michael. Cooper was his dog. I promised to take care of him while Michael was fighting in the Philippines. Everyone said I should give Cooper away after he died, but I just couldn't. He's been good company for me."

"I'm so sorry," Eve said. "Audrey and I lost our mothers in a Nazi bombing raid in London during the war."

Mrs. Herder glanced at Eve, then quickly looked away. "My ankle will heal, but I'll carry the pain of his loss until the day I die."

"I understand," Audrey said.

A second picture was also perched on the mantel, a studio photograph of a young family with three children. "Is this your family, too?" Eve asked.

"My older son, Ronald, and his wife live in Manhattan with their children."

"Will you be seeing them at Christmas?" Audrey asked.

"I don't think so. Ron is a physician like my husband was, and he finds it difficult to get away. He works in the emergency room at Lenox Hill Hospital, a very busy place."

"Might you visit him?"

Mrs. Herder sighed. "He's always asking me to take

the train into the city for a visit, but their apartment is on the tenth floor, and dogs aren't allowed. Cooper would be very unhappy boarding in a kennel."

Eve glanced at Audrey, who nodded. "If you would like to visit your son and his family for Christmas, Mrs. Herder, we would be happy to take care of Cooper for you. He could live with us while you're away."

"Families should be together during the holidays," Audrey added.

"I couldn't ask you to do that."

"You didn't ask—we're volunteering. The boys have been begging for a dog for Christmas."

"And I don't want to sound too pushy," Audrey said, "but I'll be happy to drive you to the train station, too."

"Please think it over, Mrs. Herder," Eve said. "You can let us know the next time we come to walk Cooper."

Audrey stood. "We should get going. The boys are delivering more Wise Men gifts this afternoon." Eve stood as well and glanced around for Bobby and Harry, who were ominously quiet. She found them huddled beneath the dining room table with Cooper, leafing through a magazine. "What are you reading?" she asked. They both jumped at the sound of her voice. The guilty looks on their faces made her suspicious.

She crouched down and was astonished to see it was the Sears Wish Book. "I don't believe it! Where did you get that?"

"It was on the table," Bobby said, pointing up.

"We're showing Cooper all the toys. He wanted to see them."

"He likes these fire engines," Bobby said. "The ladders really move up and down."

"Come on, it's time to go home," Eve said. "We have more gifts to deliver, remember?"

"They may keep the catalogue, if they'd like," Mrs. Herder said.

"Thank you, but we already have one at home."

"Tell us what times you would like us to walk Cooper every day," Audrey said as the boys put on their galoshes and zipped up their coats. "They're on Christmas holiday from school now."

"Well, he's used to being walked in the morning and evening, but anytime will be fine."

"And please think about our offer to watch him over the holiday," Eve said. She gestured to the boys, who were hugging the dog goodbye. "Cooper would be in very loving hands."

They all said goodbye and started for home. "Do

you think she'll take us up on our offer?" Eve asked as they walked.

"Hard to say. But honestly? I doubt it," Audrey replied.

* * *

Alan Hamilton arrived at the bungalow right on time after lunch and offered to drive everyone out to the Vandenbergs' farm in his car—a shiny new red-and-white Buick Roadmaster. "Wow!" Harry said when he saw it. "Your car looks like a candy cane!"

"Can we really ride in it, Mr. Hamilton?"

"Of course," he said, opening the rear door for them. "Hop in."

Eve scrambled into the backseat with Harry and Bobby so Audrey would have to ride in the front with Alan. Eve was certain that Audrey would scold her for it later, just as she had scolded her for inviting Alan to come with them in the first place. "I didn't invite Alan," she had reminded Audrey. "Your son did. And Alan could have politely refused, you know."

"I don't see how," Audrey had sniffed, "with everyone ganging up on him."

Tom was waiting for them in the farmyard with an ax and the sled, his light-brown hair disheveled by the wind. The sight of his handsome grin and easy stance made Eve long to run into his arms. Tom shook Alan's hand, saying, "Welcome to our farm," and patted Harry's and Bobby's heads. He gave Audrey his endearing, lopsided smile but was noticeably cool to Eve. She probably deserved it. She wanted to apologize to him for the way they had parted at the school Christmas program, but she wasn't sure how or where to begin.

"Can you pull us on the sled, Uncle Tom?" Harry asked.

"Sure thing. Climb aboard." Tom laughed and chatted with Alan as they tromped across the field through the snow to the grove of Christmas trees, pulling the sled. Tom's dog, Champ, scampered alongside them, sniffing for rabbits. It had been another hectic week at work for Eve as her boss hurried to finish all his last-minute correspondence before closing the office for three days over Christmas. She was grateful to spend her Saturday off in the sunshine and country-fresh air. But Tom's coolness chilled her heart.

Of course, Harry and Bobby chose trees that were

taller than Tom's and Alan's heads. "They need a big, *big* one!" Harry had decided with childlike generosity.

"The Robertsons' house doesn't look very large," Audrey said. "Let's see if we can find a smaller one that won't take up too much space." Eve felt a pang as Tom chopped it down, as she always did when a living tree was felled. At least it was for a good cause. They pulled the tree back to the farmhouse on the sled, then loaded everything into Tom's truck and Alan's car for the short ride to the Robertsons' house. Grandma Van came along, too.

"Now, please remember to be very polite," Audrey told the boys, "and don't say anything about how poor they are. We don't want them to be embarrassed."

"That's right," Eve added. "The three Wise Men were very rich, remember? And baby Jesus was so poor he had to sleep in a stable. So we're just going to give the Robertsons our gifts and go home again. We're not going to go inside their house or anything."

The family already knew Grandma Van, so she went up to knock on their door first, carrying a basket with homemade cinnamon rolls and a jar of her strawberry preserves. She spoke with Mrs. Robertson for a moment, then motioned for everyone else to get out of the vehicles. The Robertson boys seemed very shy at first, but when they saw Tom lifting the Christmas tree from the back of his truck and carrying it up to their house, they jumped up and down with delight. "A tree! A tree! We got a Christmas tree!"

"We thought you might like one," Grandma Van said. Tom carried the tree inside and set it up in the new stand.

"It's for Jesus' birthday!" Harry said. He hopped up and down along with the little boys. "And you can decorate it with these." He gave Mrs. Robertson the bag with the lights and tinsel and shiny balls they had purchased.

Eve watched Harry's face. He was beaming at the smaller children's expressions of delight and excitement, and she thought, *He's getting it! He sees how much fun it is to give gifts.*

"We made these chains and tinfoil stars ourselves," Bobby said, handing over the decorations they'd made last night. "And we brought you some presents too, like the Wise Men did." He was usually shy with strangers, so Eve was surprised and pleased to see him taking part. He gave Mrs. Robertson one of the toys that Tom had helped them repair, wrapped in colorful paper by

Grandma Van. Eve and Audrey and Alan made several trips from the car to the house, carrying the rest of the presents. Bobby also remembered the tin of cookies. "We helped bake them," he said.

Alan made two trips to give Mrs. Robertson the food basket from the bank, which wasn't a basket at all but a cardboard box and two grocery bags filled with food. Last of all, Eve and Audrey gave her the bags of clothes and shoes that Harry and Bobby had outgrown. The tears in Mrs. Robertson's eyes conveyed her deepest thanks.

"This is fun," Harry said after they'd said goodbye and returned to the car. "I like giving out Wise Men presents."

"Me, too!"

"Do you have time to come back to the farm for a while so the boys can go sledding?" Tom asked before climbing into his truck.

"I have a second batch of fresh cinnamon buns at home," Grandma Van called from the truck's passenger seat. "I hope you'll all come over and have some before you leave."

"Thanks, but maybe Alan needs to get back," Audrey said. "We wouldn't want to keep him."

Alan seemed amused by Audrey's protests. "I can't think of anything more important than sledding down a snowy hill and eating homemade cinnamon buns," he replied.

Eve went inside the farmhouse with Audrey and Grandma Van and watched from the kitchen window as the men pushed the boys down the sledding hill. "Why is it that our sons can be outside in the cold and the snow all day and never seem to feel a chill?" she asked.

"It's a mystery," Grandma Van said, laughing. She was pouring milk into a pot to make hot chocolate. "They seemed to have a good time delivering presents today."

"I would say that our first two Wise Men gifts were huge successes," Audrey said. She slid the pan of cinnamon buns into the warming oven for Grandma Van. "We helped Mrs. Herder shovel her sidewalk and walk her dog, and now we brought Christmas cheer to the Robertson family."

"It feels like we're getting somewhere," Eve said. She turned from the window to help start a pot of coffee. "I think the boys are learning a very important lesson."

"Do you have any ideas for your third Wise Man

gift?" Grandma asked. Eve and Audrey looked at each other.

"None whatsoever," Audrey replied. "But there are still ten days left before Christmas."

The aromas of coffee and chocolate and cinnamon filled the kitchen by the time Tom and Alan and the boys came inside, laughing and dripping melted snow. "It smells like heaven in here," Alan said, inhaling a deep whiff. Grandpa Van came in from the barn to join them.

"Well, sit down and make yourselves at home," Grandma said. "Everything is ready."

The clatter of dishes and sighs of contentment were the happiest kind of music Eve could imagine as everyone dug into the warm rolls. Home. This was what a real home should be like. She couldn't bring herself to look at Tom, knowing it would break her heart if he didn't smile back.

When it was time for everyone to leave, Tom had an announcement. "Alan and I are taking Harry and Bobby on a secret mission on Monday, if that's okay with you ladies."

Harry started bouncing up and down. "Yeah! Uncle Tom is going to pay Bobby and me to do chores so we can—"

"Shh!" Bobby put his hand over Harry's mouth. "It's a secret, remember?"

"Yeah! It's a secret!"

"We have it all planned," Tom continued. "Audrey can bring them out here for the afternoon, and I'll put them to work. Alan is meeting us downtown later for our secret errand. Then I'll bring them home in time for supper. Does that sound okay?"

"That's fine with me," Audrey replied with a smile. "I love a good mystery." Tom had asked Audrey the question, not Eve. He still seemed to be ignoring her. He didn't kiss her goodbye before she left, either. What if she had pushed Tom away one too many times?

Chapter 9

8 DAYS BEFORE CHRISTMAS

Audrey watched Eve gulp down a bowl of cornflakes for breakfast. She ate standing at the counter instead of sitting down at the table, in a rush to leave for work after spending time with Harry. "I wish I could walk Cooper with you and the boys this morning," she said between mouthfuls.

"I wish you could, too," Audrey replied. Eve always seemed to have a hard time leaving for work on Monday mornings after spending the weekend with Harry, as if she were trying to squeeze in every last minute with him.

"So I'll meet you downtown after work tonight, right?" Eve asked after taking a large swallow of her tea. They had planned to shop for presents from Santa Claus together. "Hopefully we won't run into Tom and Alan and the boys on their 'secret mission.'"

"Let me pick you up from work, Eve. It'll save you a long bus ride and we'll have more time to shop."

"Really? That would be great! Thank you!" Eve pulled on her boots, shoved her arms into her coat, and took one last mouthful of tea before hurrying out the door.

The novelty of taking Cooper for his morning walk still hadn't worn off for Harry and Bobby, and they raced through their breakfast, eager to spend time with their new friend. Cooper's entire body wagged along with his tail as he greeted them at the door. "He has really taken a liking to your boys," Mrs. Herder said.

"The feeling is mutual, believe me. Bobby has always been afraid of dogs, but he certainly loves Cooper."

After lunch, Audrey drove Bobby and Harry out to the farm for their afternoon of doing chores with Tom. They bolted from the car the moment it pulled to a stop behind the farmhouse and bounded through the snow with Tom's dog to look at the sheep. Audrey stepped from the car to greet Tom. "Thank you so much for doing this. They have been bursting with excitement all morning and asking, 'Is it time to go yet? When are we going to the farm?' I never could have imagined they'd be so eager to do chores."

"They seem to be taking their roles as Wise Men very seriously," he replied. For as long as Audrey had known Tom, he had never been without a good-natured smile, until today.

"Is everything all right?" she asked.

Tom glanced over at the boys as if to make sure they were out of earshot, then said, "Do you have a minute to talk?"

"Of course."

"It's about Eve . . ." He hesitated, chewing his lip as if he wasn't sure where to begin.

"I noticed that things seemed a little strained between you two."

"Yeah, they are. I want to talk about getting married, but she says she won't consider it until after she pays back the money she owes you. If you don't mind me prying, just how much does she owe you? Maybe I can help her out so she can pay you back sooner."

Audrey sighed. "Eve doesn't need to pay me at all! I've told her that again and again, but she won't listen. She says she lived off Robert's insurance money for four years before I came over, and that's what she's trying to repay."

"So . . . four years' worth of food, clothes, and household expenses? That adds up to quite a lot."

"The only reason I agreed to take her money in the first place was because I hoped it would help her heal. I really wish I could convince her she doesn't need to do it. But she feels so much guilt for her deception, and I think this is her way of doing penance."

"Then she probably won't take any money from me, either?"

"Probably not."

Tom exhaled and closed his eyes for a moment, his expression a mixture of anger, frustration, and sadness. "Eve also insists that she needs to stay and help you with Bobby," he said when he opened his eyes again, "and I understand that. I know you'll be going to school full-time, and you'll have a lot on your plate. But I'll be happy to help with Bobby, too. So will my parents. And I told Eve I don't mind if she keeps working after we're married if she wants to keep paying you.

I understand that you'll need her help, and I don't want to take her away from you at a bad time, but . . ." He shook his head, staring into the distance at the snowy woods beyond the pasture.

"Eve has been an enormous support to me this past year and a half as Bobby and I have gotten settled here in America. I wouldn't have known where or how to begin in a new country. I never really ran a household on my own before." She stopped, wondering for the first time if she had been leaning too heavily on Eve. Especially if it was preventing her from being with Tom.

"I have to say I'm losing hope," Tom said. "I'm beginning to think she doesn't really want to get married. Maybe she likes her independence, and so she's making all these excuses, hoping that I'll give up. If she really loved me—"

"She does love you, Tom. I know she does. But I think that deep inside, she feels as though she doesn't deserve to be happy until she pays this debt." The boys chose that moment to run back to the car, racing to see who would get there first. Harry won, of course, just as his mother always had when Eve and Audrey raced as children.

"Thanks for talking with me," Tom said, a sign that their conversation was over.

Audrey hated to see him so discouraged. She reached for his hand and squeezed it briefly. "Please let me know if I can do anything to help. I'm cheering for you, Tom."

He nodded. "I'd rather you didn't mention our conversation to Eve."

"I won't."

* * *

Tom's words haunted Audrey all afternoon after she'd returned home alone. She had some very unsettling things to think about. Mr. Barrett had offered to pay for her nurse's training—as a gift. Yet she'd decided to mortgage her house instead, in order to prove that she could get by on her own without any help. But wasn't she accepting Eve's help? Aside from Robert's life insurance money that Eve was trying to repay, Eve was also paying rent and sharing the household expenses and babysitting for Bobby. Audrey was relying on Eve's money to make ends meet while she attended college. So how, exactly, was Audrey proving her independence?

She was still mulling over these disturbing questions when she picked up Eve from work later that afternoon, and they headed into town to go Christmas shopping while the boys were with Tom and Alan. She tried to act cheerful and nonchalant so Eve wouldn't notice that anything was wrong, remembering her promise to Tom. "Shall we start with the department store?" she asked Eve. "They have a wonderful toy section." They walked up and down the toy aisles with their sons' letters to Santa Claus in hand, and she noticed Eve checking all the price tags.

"I can't decide what to buy," she said with a sigh. "I'm so worried that Harry will be disappointed, but I simply can't afford very much."

"We both decided not to indulge their greed, remember?" Audrey said. "Let's just choose two or three presents that we can afford and be done." The money in the trust fund belonged to Bobby, she told herself. As did Robert's life insurance. Like Eve, she would live only on what a single mother could afford. They decided on two shiny new steam shovels that scooped real dirt. A set of Tinkertoys for Harry and Lincoln Logs for Bobby. Then they went into Woolworth's to buy a few other little things for the boys' stockings. Audrey purchased some tape and wrapping paper and a package of invitations for Jesus' birthday party.

They had just returned home when Alan's red-and-white Buick pulled into the driveway. He got out of the car with Bobby and Harry and walked to the door with them.

Audrey went to meet him and noticed he was wearing a pin-striped suit beneath his overcoat, as if he had gone straight from work to shop with the boys. "Thanks for bringing them home," she said. "I thought Tom was going to do it."

"No problem. I offered. He has cows to milk." The boys were bouncing around Audrey and Alan as if they were so full of secrets they might burst.

"They don't seem to have run out of energy after an afternoon of work on the farm," Audrey said with a smile. "Good thing they have a dog to take for a walk in a few minutes."

Alan leaned close to whisper, "Tom and I have a bet going on how long it takes one of them to spill the beans. And another wager on which of them will do it first."

Audrey couldn't help laughing. "I'll be sure to let you know when it happens and who does it."

* * *

After walking Cooper and eating supper, the four of them sat around the dining room table to fill out the invitations to Jesus' birthday party. It was planned for three o'clock on Christmas Day. "Because Christmas is Jesus' real birthday, right, Mummy?" Bobby asked.

"That's exactly right." She was pleased that the boys made no mention of Santa Claus as they talked about what kind of birthday cake they should buy and what flavor ice cream.

"Now, who do you want to invite to this party?" Eve asked.

"You and Bobby's mommy," Harry replied.

"Yes, thank you. We'll be very happy to attend."

"Nana and Granddad Barrett," Bobby said.

"And Grandma and Grandpa Van and Uncle Tom," Harry added.

"And Mr. Hamilton," Bobby said.

"Mr. Hamilton may be busy with his family on Christmas Day," Audrey said quickly.

"But we still can ask him," Eve said just as quickly.

Audrey would need to talk to Eve after the boys went to bed about making sure the boys didn't become too attached to Alan. Eve was wrong to keep pushing him into their lives this way, as if he could take Robert's place in Bobby's life. Or hers.

"What about Mrs. Herder and Cooper?" Bobby asked. "Can we invite them?"

"Yeah, she doesn't even have a Christmas tree," Harry said.

"Well, you can give her an invitation when you see her tomorrow," Eve replied. "We would have to pick her up in our car. She has a sprained ankle, remember?"

"I don't want you boys to be too disappointed if she refuses," Audrey said, "but it is very sweet of you to think of her."

Audrey wrote out all the invitations while Eve addressed the envelopes. Bobby and Harry printed their own names on the bottom of each one and licked the envelopes and the three-cent stamps. "We'll put them in the mailbox tomorrow," Eve promised.

"There's one more thing we should talk about before bedtime," Audrey said as they moved into the living room to watch television. "We need to decide what we're going to do for our third Wise Man gift. There are only eight days left until Christmas. Any ideas?"

"You boys did a great job on the first two gifts," Eve said, bending to give Harry a hug. "Mrs. Herder and the Robertson family were very grateful for your gifts. And we're so proud of you for working so hard."

"It was fun! We like being Wise Men," Harry replied.

"Does the gift have to go to people we don't know?" Bobby asked.

"I don't think so. Why?"

"I want to buy a present for everyone we invited to the party. We can't have a birthday party without presents."

Audrey gazed at her son, touched by his generosity and thoughtfulness. She bent to kiss his forehead. "I think that's a wonderful third gift from our little Wise Men."

"Make a list, Mummy." Bobby held up his fingers as he counted off the names. "One for Nana and Granddad and Grandma and Grandpa Van and Uncle Tom and Mr. Hamilton . . ."

"We don't need to buy presents for you, Mommy, because—"

Bobby socked Harry in the shoulder, cutting him off. "Shh! It's a secret, remember?"

Audrey covered her mouth to hide a smile,

remembering the wager between Alan and Tom. She would have put her money on Harry being the bean spiller.

"Okay, okay," Harry said with a sigh.

"Do you have some chores we could do around the house, Mummy?" Bobby asked.

"Yeah, we're going to need more money so we can pay for all these presents. We already spent the money we earned out at the farm on—"

Bobby socked him again. "Shh!"

"Sorry. I keep forgetting."

Audrey looked at Eve and smiled. "They're really getting the idea. Yes, of course you can earn some money helping around the house. We'll think up a list of chores you can do, starting tomorrow. Then we'll all go shopping next Saturday because Harry's mum won't have to work."

Audrey sat down on the sofa with Eve after the boys were in bed. "Can you help me think of some chores they can do over the next few days?" she asked.

"I can think of a few." Eve moved closer to Audrey and lowered her voice. "But how are we going to pay the boys for doing them? I'm just about broke, Audrey, and we still have to buy the cake and ice cream, too."

"I've been thinking about that, and I've decided that I'm giving you back your rent money for this month—"

"Audrey, no! I can't let you do that!"

"I don't care if you 'let' me do it or not—I'm doing it. We're trying to teach the boys about giving, aren't we? Well, let me give this gift to you. Just this once."

"Okay. But if there's any money left over after we pay for the party and the gifts, I want you to apply it toward the rent. Is it a deal?" Audrey saw how badly Eve needed her to agree.

"It's a deal." She stood to turn on the television, then thought of something. "Before I forget, I need to put Mrs. Herder's invitation where I'll remember to bring it to her when the boys walk Cooper in the morning." Audrey went into the kitchen and propped it on the counter by the teapot. "It makes me so sad to think of Mrs. Herder sitting all alone at Christmas," she said when she returned to the living room. "But I'm guessing she won't come to the birthday party. She doesn't know us very well."

"I hope she'll take us up on our offer to watch Cooper so she can visit her son."

"I do, too, but I'm not holding my breath."

Eve suddenly sat upright on the couch. "Maybe we need to give her a little nudge."

Audrey could almost see the little gears spinning in Eve's brain and braced herself for one of her bold ideas. "I'm afraid to ask, but what sort of nudge do you have in mind?"

"We should call Mrs. Herder's son in New York City. If we tell him about our offer to watch Cooper, maybe he can coax her to accept, and she can spend Christmas with her family."

"I don't know, Eve. Don't you think we might be meddling just a bit too much?"

"The worst that could happen is that Mrs. Herder gets mad at us for interfering and never speaks to us again. But it's Christmas, Audrey. I hate to think of her sitting home all alone. She should be with her children and grandchildren."

"How would you ever find her son?"

"Well, we know his name is Dr. Ronald Herder and that he works at Lenox Hill Hospital. We could just try phoning him."

"At the emergency room?"

"Why not? We can say that it has to do with his

mother. We'll ask if he knows that she fell on the ice. It's a very legitimate reason for the call."

"What if he panics and fears the worst? We don't want to frighten the poor man when he receives a telephone call about his mum from a stranger."

Eve waved away her concerns. "He works in an emergency room. He's probably used to surprises."

Audrey could tell that Eve wasn't going to let the idea go. She was like Cooper with his ball—once he got it between his teeth, he wouldn't drop it.

"Dr. Herder may not even know that his mother fell and hurt herself," Eve continued. "You can start by telling him that, and once you have his attention, you can tell him about our offer to watch Cooper."

"Wait . . . after *I* have his attention?"

"I'm giving this job to you, Audrey. I would call him myself, but I'll be at work all day."

Audrey opened her mouth to protest and to insist that Eve follow through with this crazy idea herself but halted. She thought of her conversation with Tom and the unsettling conclusion she'd reached that she relied too heavily on Eve. She didn't want to be the reason that Eve was making Tom wait. Audrey exhaled, knowing that she would have to be the one to call Dr. Herder. "I still think we may be meddling a bit too much."

"It's Christmas. And like Harry says, 'We're the smart kings.'"

* * *

Audrey walked past the telephone stand in the hallway several times the next morning as she tried to summon the courage to call Mrs. Herder's son. After the boys had taken Cooper for his walk, she had sent them outside and assigned the first of their moneymaking chores— clearing the dusting of snow that had fallen overnight from the driveway. By the time they finished rolling in it, shoveling it, and pitching snowballs at each other, it would probably be lunchtime.

Calling a stranger—a busy doctor, no less—wasn't something that Audrey was comfortable doing. Yet Eve had been encouraging her to do difficult tasks all of her life, beginning with the very first time they met and Eve had convinced Audrey to stand up to her parents about attending boarding school. Eve had given Audrey dead beetles to hold to help her overcome her fears. She had been bolstering Audrey's courage for the past year and a half, helping her get settled in America and taking the necessary steps to attend college. Was it time now to stand on her own two feet? To live here in her bungalow alone with Bobby?

The idea frightened her. But Audrey decided she needed to help Eve. And Tom, who had been waiting patiently all this time. Audrey remembered an incident during their military training when Eve's claustrophobia nearly prevented her from passing the required gas-mask test. Audrey had taken Eve by the hand and led her panicked friend out of the chamber so they could both pass the test. True, they were meddling in Mrs. Herder's life by telephoning her son. And Eve had been meddling in Audrey's life by inviting Alan Hamilton everywhere. Maybe Audrey should meddle in Eve's and Tom's lives, for once. But first she would have to figure out how.

Audrey glanced out the window to see if the boys were still shoveling, then picked up the phone and a pen. Directory assistance gave her the number for the hospital switchboard. She told the receptionist whom she wanted to speak with and waited for her to transfer the call to the emergency room. The longer Audrey waited, the higher the fee for the long-distance call would be on her next telephone bill. She hoped it would be worth it. Audrey liked Mrs. Herder. She could understand her lingering grief over the loss of her son. Not a day went by that Audrey didn't think about Robert.

At last, the emergency room nurse picked up. Audrey asked if Dr. Herder was on duty and if she could speak with him. She half hoped that he wasn't because her courage was slowly draining away, but it turned out that he was on duty. It seemed like a small miracle.

"May I say who's calling?" the nurse asked.

"Mrs. Robert Barrett. I'm his mother's neighbor in Connecticut." She waited again, hearing the clock ticking and the long-distance charges adding up.

Finally he answered. "This is Dr. Herder."

"Hello, Doctor. My name is Audrey Barrett, and I'm one of your mother's neighbors. I'm not sure if she's told you or not, but she fell on the ice a few days ago and sprained her ankle and her wrist."

"No, I didn't know. Is she all right?"

"Yes, just a little lame. My friend and I have been looking in on her and taking Cooper for his walks every day until she's better—"

"That's very nice of you. Thank you."

She heard several excited voices in the background. A telephone ringing. Distant sirens wailing. They brought back memories of racing to emergency rooms in her ambulance. Dr. Herder was surely a busy man.

She drew another breath and hurried on, not giving him a chance to get angry with her for interfering. "Now, I realize that this sounds very forward of me, and I hope you won't think I'm being a nosy neighbor, but your mother mentioned that she is unable to be with you and your family over the Christmas holiday because of her dog, and so I wanted to tell you that my friend and I have offered to take Cooper home to our house for Christmas so your mother can visit you. My son is five years old and he just adores the dog. We all do." Audrey halted, wincing. She sounded like a gushing, meddlesome busybody. She waited for the doctor to say something. The sirens in the background grew louder.

"And my mother agreed to this?"

"Well, not exactly. We were hoping you could convince her. Families really should be together at Christmas."

"I . . . um . . . Thank you, Mrs. . . . ?"

"Barrett. Audrey Barrett."

"Yes. Thank you for letting me know about Mother. And about the dog."

"You're very welcome. And please—" But he had already rung off.

She spent the rest of the morning worrying, wondering if she'd done the right thing. She continued to worry all afternoon as the boys cleaned out the front coat closet for her and helped her shop for groceries. They were quite proud of themselves for carrying the grocery bags inside all by themselves. Then it was time to take Cooper for his afternoon walk, and she worried all the way there, fearing that Mrs. Herder would be angry with her. The boys would be devastated if she slammed the door in their faces. But no, surely the busy doctor wouldn't have had time to call his mother, yet.

Mrs. Herder did look quite stern when she answered her door. Cooper didn't have his leash on. "Come in for a minute," she said. Audrey obeyed, telling the boys to wait on the porch. "You telephoned my son," Mrs. Herder said without preamble.

"Yes. I hope you aren't angry with us. We just wanted to help you and Cooper."

"I was annoyed, yes. But Ronald convinced me that you meant well."

Audrey waited, holding her breath. "So have you decided to go?" she asked when she couldn't wait any longer.

"I wasn't going to at first, because the train would be too difficult to manage with my lame ankle. But my son insists on driving up here to fetch me tomorrow. It's his day off."

"That's wonderful! I'm so pleased to hear it!" Audrey could breathe again. "And the boys will be thrilled to be able to take Cooper home. What time shall we come to get him tomorrow?" She hoped it would be in the evening so Eve could meet Dr. Herder and see the happy result of her meddling. But Mrs. Herder said he would be arriving around noon.

Bobby and Harry were so excited by the news that Cooper was coming to stay for a few days that they were scarcely able to fall asleep. The next day, Audrey walked over to Mrs. Herder's house with the boys just before noon. She thought something seemed different about Mrs. Herder's house as she came up the front walk to knock on the door, but it took her a moment to realize what it was. The gold star that had announced to the world that Mrs. Herder had lost her son in the war was no longer in the front window.

Audrey was trying to decide whether to comment on it or not when the door opened and Mrs. Herder greeted them, dressed in a gray wool traveling suit and matching hat. She had always seemed so solemn and reserved to Audrey, but today she had a smile on her face. "Do you have time to come in?" she asked. "I have all of Cooper's things ready to go—his food, his favorite chew toys, his water and food dishes. And his brush. He likes to be brushed every day." Her love for the dog was very clear. "I would like for you to stay and meet my son and his family, if you have the time."

"Of course. I would love to meet them. Maybe the boys can play fetch with Cooper in the backyard until he arrives. They're being very rambunctious today." And it would give Audrey a chance to ask Mrs. Herder about the absent gold star.

"Cooper would like that. His ball is in this bag, too."

"I'll walk around to the backyard with them to make sure the gate is shut tight. I'll be right back." Dr. Herder still hadn't arrived when Audrey returned, so she decided to take a chance as they sat together in Mrs. Herder's gracious living room. "I couldn't help noticing that the gold star is no longer in your front window," she began.

Mrs. Herder gave a curt nod. "I took it down. It was time." She looked over at the family photographs on the mantel and then back at Audrey. "It's natural to mourn the people we love and to cling to them in our memory. But there comes a time when it's also natural to be happy again. It doesn't mean that we loved them any less. In fact, I think it's a sign of our great love for them that we can still remember what love feels like and be willing to give it and receive it once again."

Audrey swallowed a knot of grief. Mrs. Herder was talking about herself, but her words were an arrow that pierced Audrey's heart.

"Eve told me that the two of you lost loved ones, too," she continued.

"Y-yes. We both lost our mothers in the Blitz. And my husband, Robert. Not in the war but in an automobile accident after he had returned home."

Mrs. Herder smiled. "You're still so young. I hope you won't be afraid to love again."

Audrey paused. "I think that in many ways, I have been afraid." She couldn't deny how hard she'd fought all of Eve's efforts to include Alan in their activities.

"I've been afraid, as well, dear. But it's time for me to face my fear. And I hope it's time for you and Eve,

169

too. I took the star down because I realized how wrong it was for me to turn my grief into a shrine. To hang my sorrow in a prominent place where it was visible for everyone to see how very much I loved my son. But it doesn't mean that I love him any less now that I've tucked the star away, at last."

"That was very courageous of you."

"Not at all. It was cowardly of me to keep it there. I knew that it would keep everyone at a distance from me, because they would be afraid to intrude on my grief. I didn't have to open my heart to love again. Then your friend Eve waltzed through my door one day, followed soon after by you and the boys, and everything changed. I'd had the foolish notion that Cooper was mourning for Michael, too. It was just the two of us, living here in our loneliness and grief. But then I saw how quickly Cooper warmed up to your boys. I haven't seen him this happy in years. It doesn't mean that Cooper didn't love his master. He can love Harry and Bobby and still love Michael. And I can, too." She leaned forward and took both of Audrey's hands. "You and Eve and your sons gave Cooper and me your love as a gift, reminding us of what we've been missing."

Tears filled Audrey's eyes. What if Eve hadn't meddled

by knocking on Mrs. Herder's door that first day? What if she hadn't meddled by insisting that Audrey call Dr. Herder? And what if Eve hadn't meddled by inviting Alan Hamilton to be part of their lives this Christmas?

"I've been punishing myself by not visiting Ronald and his family at Christmas," Mrs. Herder said, "because it seemed wrong to be happy and to celebrate together if Michael couldn't be with us. As if I should never be happy or celebrate Christmas again. How ridiculous of me! If I engage wholeheartedly with life again, it doesn't mean that I didn't love Michael. Am I making any sense?"

Audrey nodded as tears rolled down her cheeks.

"Oh, now I've gone and made you cry. I'm sorry."

"Don't be. My tears are because you've made me realize that I've been doing the same thing. I've also built a shrine to my husband's memory, and I've barricaded myself inside, trying to keep everything exactly as we had planned before he died and to live the way I thought he would have wanted. My son asked Santa Claus to bring him a daddy for Christmas, and it made me furious, as if Bobby was being disloyal to my husband to think of ever wanting another father. You and Cooper have shown me how wrong I was to feel that way. Thank you. I'll have a lot to think about in the days ahead."

Footsteps clomped across the front porch, and the door opened out in the hallway, startling them both. "Hello . . . Mom . . . ?" a cheery voice called. Audrey and Mrs. Herder both stood as three children ran past the man in the doorway to hug their grandmother. How Audrey wished that Eve could be here to see this happy reunion. She wiped her tears as Mrs. Herder introduced her to the grandchildren and to her son and daughter-in-law.

"Thank you so much for calling me," Dr. Herder said. "And for offering to watch the dog."

"I'm very glad I did."

"Here's the key to my house if you wouldn't mind keeping an eye on it," Mrs. Herder said.

"I would be happy to. And we'll bring in your mail, too."

"I can help you walk to the car, Grandma," the granddaughter said, hugging Mrs. Herder's waist. Her two grandsons helped load her suitcase and some Christmas parcels into the car.

Harry and Bobby ran to the gate with the dog to wave goodbye. "We'll take real good care of Cooper for you," Harry called.

"Thank you. I know you will, dear boy."

Audrey stood on the porch to wave goodbye as Dr. Herder's car pulled away. Then she fastened Cooper to his leash, gathered up his doggy things, and locked the door behind her. She turned to look back at the house again when she reached the sidewalk, still amazed to see that the gold star was really gone. And in that moment, she knew a small crack had opened up in the wall of the shrine that she'd built for Robert—not a huge one, but perhaps it was wide enough for Alan Hamilton to squeeze through.

The boys galloped down the street ahead of Audrey, with Cooper straining on his leash. "Yippee!" Harry cheered. "We got a dog for Christmas!"

Chapter 10

"I wonder how long it will take me to get used to having a dog around the house," Audrey said the next evening after supper. "I've tripped over his water dish twice already and had to mop up the mess." She sat in the living room with Eve after they'd given the boys their baths, browsing through the latest issue of *Life* magazine. The lights on their Christmas tree made the room feel cozy, even if there weren't any presents beneath it.

"That reminds me," Eve said. "Our Christmas tree is going to need watering every day. Cooper keeps sticking his big head under there and slurping it all up."

"He is a bit too big for our bungalow, isn't he?" Audrey replied. "Where is he, by the way?"

"In the bedroom with the boys. They're being suspiciously quiet, don't you think? And they're not clamoring to watch television for once."

Audrey listened for a moment. Hearing nothing, she lifted the magazine to continue reading. She had just turned the page when Harry and Bobby trotted into the living room with smiles on their faces and Cooper at their heels.

"Mummy, can we please have the Wish Book again?" Bobby asked.

"Tell me why, first."

"Because Santa Claus is going to be at the Christmas party tomorrow, and we need to tell him we changed our minds."

"It's a little too late for that," Eve said. "Christmas is in five days. Santa probably has his sleigh all loaded up and ready to go by now."

Audrey saw Bobby's disappointed expression and brushed his damp hair off his forehead. "What did you want to change, love?"

"Well, when we went shopping with Uncle Tom and Mr. Hamilton, we saw that big airplane in the store window again, and we remembered that we really, really wanted it."

"And it's not on our list," Harry added.

"If it's in the store, why do you need the Wish Book?" Eve asked.

"Because when we see Santa at the party tomorrow, and we tell him we want the airplane, we'll need to tell him what he can cross off our list."

Their attitude touched Audrey. What a change from two weeks earlier when they'd first discovered the Wish Book. She rose from her chair and fetched it from where she'd hidden it in the china cabinet. "Thanks, Mummy!" The boys raced back to their bedroom with Cooper right behind them.

"That dog seems to think he's their little brother," Eve said.

Audrey smiled and sank down on the sofa again with a satisfied sigh. "It's so encouraging to see how much their attitude about asking for toys has changed, isn't it?"

Eve leaned toward Audrey, speaking softly. "Yes, except that I already bought Harry's presents. I can't afford that airplane. Did you see how big it was? It was in the store window with all those shiny aluminum pots and pans and percolators. I'm sure it's very expensive."

"I agree. We can't afford it. Maybe they'll forget all about it by Christmas." Yet the thought occurred to Audrey that she *could* afford it. She'd been reminded of how much money was in her trust fund account when she'd applied for the bank loan. She could afford to buy an airplane for each of the boys. But what would Robert say about such an extravagance? He had wanted to live simply, without relying on his inherited wealth. She pushed away the thought of splurging. "I'm glad the boys mentioned the party at the country club tomorrow. I had forgotten all about it."

"I'm glad that I have to work tomorrow and can't go. It's such a stuffy event with everyone all dressed up—mothers, grandmothers, and the children, too. I have no idea why. How can anyone enjoy a party while wearing clothes that are all stiff and itchy? And you know the boys are going to drip chocolate ice cream all over their Sunday clothes. Why not let them wear corduroys and polo shirts?"

"I think most mothers enjoy dressing up their little girls in ribbons and bows and lace," Audrey replied. "It's different with boys, I suppose."

"Thank heaven I have a boy!" Eve glanced at her, grinning, but Audrey didn't feel much like smiling.

"Uh-oh. You've got that worry crease between your eyebrows again. Don't tell me you're nervous about tomorrow's party?"

"Not the party, but I've been thinking that I should tell Mrs. Barrett about my date with Alan on Friday night. I'm worried she'll find out about it some other way—you know how chummy those country-club people are."

"Some of those women have nothing better to do than spread gossip. And a handsome, eligible bachelor like Alan Hamilton is certainly worthy of gossip."

"I think Mrs. Barrett should hear the news about Alan from me first. Even though he's *only* a friend and it isn't *really* a date. But I don't quite know how to tell her."

"I don't think it's any of her business."

"Maybe not," Audrey said with a sigh. "It's just that Mr. Barrett was upset that I went behind his back to apply for the loan. Neither of them is happy about my nursing career. We may have insulted them further by asking them not to buy so many toys. I just don't want to do anything else to make them upset with me."

"You worry too much."

"What if they think I'm being disloyal to their son by dating someone?"

"Do *you* feel like you're being disloyal?"

The question hit Audrey square in her chest. She didn't want to consider it, much less answer it. Maybe the crack in her shrine wasn't wide enough for Alan to squeeze through after all. "I feel I should explain to Mrs. Barrett that Alan and I are just friends."

"Do whatever you think is best, Audrey. But please remember that Robert made a deliberate choice *not* to live his life according to his parents' expectations. We're bound to disappoint people, but we can't let it influence our decisions. And just so you know, you're going to disappoint me and probably Bobby, too, if you don't give Alan Hamilton a chance."

*   *   *

The Christmas party at the country club turned out to be a happy, festive affair with an enormous Christmas tree festooned with colorful lights and plenty of activities to keep the children entertained. Audrey was glad for the boys' sakes, and for her mother-in-law's, that she had come. Bobby and Harry joined in all the games and even managed to win a few prizes. There was a puppet show with marionettes. Clowns doing pranks and magic tricks. A real-live reindeer for the children to pet. And enough cake and ice cream and candy to give the boys tummy aches for a week. A photographer with a Polaroid instant camera took pictures of them as they sat on Santa's lap to tell him their Christmas wishes. Afterwards, Santa gave each child a puppet from one of the boys' favorite television shows, *Howdy Doody*.

Audrey didn't have a chance to speak privately with Mrs. Barrett until late in the afternoon when they were sitting at their table alone, enjoying tea and coffee. The boys had already finished their cake and ice cream and had run off to watch the clowns perform. Audrey summoned her courage and faced her mother-in-law. "I thought you should know that . . . that I've become friends with Alan Hamilton. He's their Boys' Club leader at church, and he's been helping us with some charity projects for Christmas, and . . . well, he has invited me to attend a Christmas party with him tomorrow night for the bank employees, and I agreed to go. I was worried that you might feel it was too soon and—"

"Too soon?" Mrs. Barrett arched her brows in surprise. Her dark eyes were so much like Robert's, especially when they sparkled with delight.

"Yes. I loved Robert very much—"

Mrs. Barrett's warm laughter interrupted her. She reached for Audrey's hand and held it between hers. "My dear, I can only say it's about time."

Audrey felt a wave of relief. Did Mrs. Barrett really feel that way? Audrey thought again about the gold star in Mrs. Herder's window and her words about turning her grief into a shrine.

"There's no need at all to worry about us, Audrey. We want your happiness—and Bobby's. Alan is a wonderful young man."

"You know him, then?"

She laughed again. "Alan's mother, Priscilla, and I are longtime friends. We've often said that if we could wish for a lovely match, it would be for the two of you to find each other."

"You haven't been playing matchmaker, have you?" Audrey wasn't sure if she should be angry or pleased.

"Nothing of the sort. We did nothing to interfere. But Priscilla did telephone me after Alan raved on and on about how strong and independently minded you were. She said it was the first time Alan has shown an interest in any woman since his wife died. And we were very pleased, as well."

"His wife? I-I didn't realize Alan had been married." Why hadn't he mentioned it? Audrey couldn't have said why the news had rattled her, but it did.

Mrs. Barrett took a sip of coffee and set down her cup. "It was very tragic. His wife was ill for quite some time and passed away not long after our Robert died. Priscilla and I consoled each other."

Her words should have relieved Audrey, but they brought a host of new concerns. How could she live up to another wife's memory? Not to mention all of their parents' combined expectations. "Listen, I hope you and Mrs. Hamilton won't pin your hopes too high for Alan and me," she said. "At least not just yet. It's much too soon to know if . . . I mean, we hardly know each other."

"I understand. But if you should decide that you're fond of each other, you would certainly have our blessing."

"Thank you. That means so much." This was happening too fast. Much too fast. Audrey knew she was still keeping her gold star of grief very visible for all to see. She wasn't ready to put it away as Mrs. Herder had, afraid that all her memories of Robert would begin to fade if she did.

"I hope you enjoy your dinner tomorrow night," Mrs. Barrett said. "And that for as long as your new friendship with Alan lasts, you'll both think of it as a special Christmas gift."

Audrey had given Nana Barrett a ride to the party, and by the time she drove her home and the boys had showered her with kisses and hugs to thank her for the party, the day was fading. Eve was already home from work. "That must have been some party," she said as they all tumbled inside. "The boys look as if they're arriving home from war."

Audrey had to laugh when she looked at Harry and Bobby with their shirttails out, their clothes wrinkled and smeared with ice cream, their lips and tongues stained purple from grape-flavored candy. Their pockets bulged, and their arms were loaded down with bags of prizes and presents. Cooper danced in happy circles around them as they came inside, his tail sweeping like a pendulum, his pink tongue licking their sticky faces.

"That was the best party ever!" Harry said. He dumped his loot on the kitchen table and ran to Eve, who crouched down for a hug.

"I'm so glad you enjoyed it."

"Santa gave everybody a puppet for Christmas," he

said. "Bobby got Howdy Doody and I got Clarabell the clown!"

"They're wound up so tightly I don't know how we'll ever get them to settle down," Audrey said.

"I do," Eve said. "It's time to take Cooper for a walk."

* * *

The following evening, Audrey's nerves were jingling like Christmas bells as she stood in her slip in front of her clothes closet, getting ready for her date with Alan. She turned to Eve, who was sitting on one of their twin beds, watching her get ready. "I never should have agreed to this date. If you called Alan right now and told him I have a stomachache and can't go with him tonight, it wouldn't be a lie."

"I'll do no such thing. And I won't even comment on how ridiculous you're being." Eve stood and went to the closet. "We need to decide what you're going to wear."

"Now that I know the Barretts and Hamiltons are friends, and that they have great hopes for Alan and me, there's even more pressure weighing on this date."

"But don't you see? Alan is probably sensing the

same pressure you are. He'll know exactly how you feel. You'll have something to laugh about together."

"I don't feel much like laughing."

"Let me pick a dress for you." Hangers scraped along the clothes bar as Eve riffled through Audrey's clothes. "Here. I love this dark-blue dress on you. It shows off your tiny waist and makes you look like Grace Kelly." Eve held it up in front of Audrey. The dress was made of midnight-blue satin and had a modest, square neck and cap sleeves. Audrey would have to wear her crinoline under the full, flared skirt. "With a pair of elbow-length gloves and a string of pearls, it'll be perfect. What time is Alan coming?"

"Six o'clock. Don't forget—I need you to take the boys and Cooper for a walk before he gets here. I don't want Bobby to make too much of this date."

"I think it's a little late to worry about that," Eve said with a grin. "Bobby already asked Alan to be his daddy, remember?"

Audrey clutched her head. "How can I forget? I was so embarrassed!"

"But don't worry. I'll make sure Bobby is gone when Alan comes."

Audrey sat down at the dressing table to put on her

makeup while Eve removed the bobby pins from her pin curls so she could brush her hair. "Isn't it fun to get all dressed up to go dancing again?" Eve asked.

"I wish I'd never spoken to Mrs. Barrett about Alan."

"Audrey, listen to me." She gripped Audrey's shoulders and met her gaze in the mirror. "I know for a fact that you've enjoyed yourself these past few weeks when we've been with Alan—decorating our Christmas tree, going to the school program, cutting down the tree out at Tom's farm, and delivering presents to the Robertson family. For once in your life, please stop worrying and fretting and just enjoy yourself. Enjoy being with him. Alan is our friend. And it's Christmas!"

"You need to stop saying, 'It's Christmas.' I know it's Christmas."

"Then think of this evening as an early Christmas present." It was what Mrs. Barrett had said, as well— that she should think of her friendship with Alan as a gift. *That's all it is,* she told herself. *A friendship.* When the holiday season ended, their friendship would likely become a mere memory, tossed out with the tree and the tinsel and the wrapping paper.

The boys were sitting on the floor with Cooper, watching television, when Audrey emerged from her bedroom, ready to go. "Oh, Mummy!" Bobby said. "You look like a princess!" And Bobby looked so much like Robert, from his dark hair and eyes, right down to the cleft in his chin.

"Thank you, sweet boy." She bent to kiss his forehead, then glanced at the clock—almost six. "I think it's time to take Cooper for his walk, isn't it?" The dog understood the word *walk*, and he stood and twirled in a circle, tail thumping against the sofa. Thankfully, the novelty of having a dog still hadn't worn off, and the boys jumped up to put on their coats and galoshes.

Alan arrived a short time later with a beautiful corsage of red roses. "You look lovely tonight, Audrey," he told her as he helped her fasten it to her wrist.

"Thank you." She got a whiff of his cologne as he held her coat. She felt a jitter of nerves ripple through her stomach, but then Alan smiled—and there was something about his appealing, one-sided dimple that put her at ease. Eve was right. This was their friend Alan. She needed to simply enjoy the evening with her friend. How many years had it been since she'd danced with anyone?

"Before I forget," Alan said, "please tell Bobby and Harry that I received their invitation, and I would be happy to come to their birthday party for Jesus on Christmas Day. I was hoping they'd be here so I could tell them myself."

"They're walking our neighbor's dog at the moment, but they'll be very glad to hear it."

The dining room at the country club had been transformed after yesterday's children's party into a lovely, winter fairyland with candles and fragrant pine boughs and thousands of twinkling lights. Audrey felt a brief moment of panic when Alan introduced her to his parents, wondering if she would measure up to his first wife. Audrey's experiences with dating had always meant being analyzed and sized up by parents on both sides, who would decide if she measured up. She knew that Mrs. Barrett and Mrs. Hamilton already approved of this match, but instead of offering relief, it brought a new worry. Would their mothers push too hard? As another jitter of nerves rippled through her stomach, Audrey could almost hear Eve whispering in her ear and saying, "Stop worrying!" And Eve was right.

Audrey drew a steadying breath and smiled as she spoke with Mrs. Hamilton for a few minutes. Then she held Alan's arm as he made the rounds during the cocktail hour, greeting his bank employees and their spouses and dates. She wondered what she and Alan looked like together. He was so tall and solidly built, while she was small-boned and petite. Alan had a way of making everyone feel comfortable and welcome as he chatted with them, and his good nature soon had the same effect on Audrey. She managed to stop worrying and felt relaxed and at ease by the time they took their seats at their table.

Alan was charming and attentive as they ate their way through the elaborate dinner, asking what she liked about America and what she missed about home. He seemed fascinated by her accounts of driving an ambulance during the war.

"Now it's your turn," she said before dessert was served. "Were you in the service during the war?"

"I enlisted in the army, but my job wasn't nearly as exciting as yours. I was based in Washington, DC, for almost the entire time and traveled around the country as a liaison between Uncle Sam and various businesses that had government contracts. Very boring, really, compared to what you did."

"But quite necessary. I know firsthand how valuable all of those tanks and weapons were when it came to saving my homeland."

"I never did get to see Europe or Asia like most of my friends," he said with a sigh, "but I did travel around America quite a bit. And it was fortunate that my wife was able to live with me in Washington during the war."

Audrey had been searching for a way to ask about his wife and was grateful that he'd provided an opening. "Mrs. Barrett told me you'd been married. I would love to hear about your wife, if you don't mind."

He nodded but looked down at the table and toyed with his dessert fork as he spoke. "I met Elizabeth when I was in college and she was studying at Vassar. She was my roommate's younger sister. I think we both knew we were in love from the very beginning, and we made plans to get married after we graduated. But then the Japanese attacked Pearl Harbor and I decided to enlist. When I finished all of my military training and learned that I would be posted in Washington, we decided to forget about the great, big wedding we'd planned and just get married in a simple church ceremony."

"Robert and I were married in my hospital room after I was injured by a V-1 rocket," Audrey said, remembering. "My wedding gown was a hospital gown. It's funny how the things we'd always imagined were important, like a fancy wedding, turn out to be not so important after all."

"That's true. And I'm very glad that Lizzie and I didn't wait. Not long after our third wedding anniversary, she was diagnosed with Hodgkin's disease. It advanced very quickly. Just over a year later, she was gone."

"I'm so sorry."

"I know I don't need to tell you what it's been like to grieve a loss like that. You understand all too well. I'm grateful for the time Lizzie and I had together—more time than you had with Robert, I'm guessing."

"You're right. And we were apart for much of that time. But I thank God every day that we had Bobby."

"And now Bobby seems to have brought us together," Alan said with a smile. He reached for her hand as the band began playing "The Tennessee Waltz" and asked, "Would you care to dance, Audrey? Lizzie always accused me of having two left feet, but I think I can manage a waltz."

"I would love to." He led her to the dance floor and took her in his arms. Audrey closed her eyes as they swayed to the music. Holding Alan was very different from holding Robert, who had been slender and not nearly as muscular as Alan. But oh, how wonderful it was to be held in a man's arms again. She felt the crack in her shrine to Robert opening just a little bit more.

"I want to talk about happier things, Audrey, but before we do, I want to thank you for including me in all your Christmas activities. It has been such a gift to me." There were those words again—*a gift*.

"We've enjoyed having you with us." It was true, even if Eve had been the one who kept insisting that he join them.

"Ever since Lizzie died, I've been trying to bury my grief beneath piles of work. But spending time with you and the boys has made me want to enjoy life again. I know that you understand the pain of loving . . . and also the fear that if you love someone new, you'll risk the pain of grief all over again. I haven't been ready to take that risk yet."

"Neither have I. Robert was gone before I even had a chance to say goodbye."

"For Lizzie and me, it was a very long, very difficult goodbye."

"I suppose there's no easy way to lose someone you love," Audrey said softly.

"This is the first time that I've enjoyed Christmas

in years. Reaching out to the Robertson family felt wonderful. I admire what you and Eve are teaching Bobby and Harry about giving. And I want you to know that one of the people your little Wise Men gave a gift to was me." The song had ended, but Alan pulled her close for a brief hug. "Thank you."

She smiled up at him. "You're very welcome." They remained on the dance floor, holding hands, and it seemed perfectly natural to begin dancing again as the band started playing "Because of You."

"I hope we can spend more time together as friends in the coming year," he said. "I've needed a good friend who understands the toll that grief takes. What do you say?"

He gazed down at her, and Audrey thought she understood how Mrs. Herder must have felt as she removed the gold star from her window. There was a lingering shadow of guilt and regret, as if she were saying a final goodbye to a familiar friend, but also a sliver of hope and anticipation. "I would like that very much, Alan."

He waltzed her to the middle of the floor, and when one of the other couples began laughing and pointing to the ceiling, she looked at the chandelier above their heads. A green branch was dangling from it. "I believe that's mistletoe," Alan said with a smile. He held Audrey by the shoulders and bent to kiss her. The warmth and joy of it spread all the way to Audrey's toes. "That was just a friendly kiss, of course," he said afterwards, trying to look serious.

"Of course," Audrey said, trying to appear equally serious. Then she smiled and added, "But I still enjoyed it."

Chapter 11

4 DAYS BEFORE CHRISTMAS

Eve couldn't concentrate on any of the programs on television. She couldn't stop thinking about Audrey's dinner date with Alan, wondering how it was going, whether Audrey was able to relax for once and stop her endless worrying long enough to enjoy herself. Bobby had been right—his mother had looked like a princess. Sleeping Beauty, perhaps? Eve hoped Audrey would finally awaken and take a chance at love again.

She had tucked the boys into bed thirty minutes ago, but she could still hear them whispering and giggling. They would probably find it even harder to fall asleep on Christmas Eve. They had begged to have the dog sleep with them on the first night, which was out of the question considering how big Cooper was. But Eve and Audrey had finally agreed to allow him to sleep on a rug next to their bunks. "But not on the bed, please. There won't be any room for either of you."

The tinsel on the Christmas tree glowed like multi-colored icicles, reflecting the lights. The space beneath it was still empty. How Eve wished that Harry could wake up on Christmas morning to find piles of toys beneath it—everything he'd asked for in the Wish Book along with the big aluminum airplane from the store window. If only she could afford it. Was it too late to ask Nana Barrett to buy the airplane for him? And would Audrey be angry with her if she did?

Eve stood to change the television channel and saw a pair of headlights arc across the front window as a ve-hicle pulled into the driveway. It couldn't be Audrey and Alan back so soon, could it? But then she recognized the familiar rattle and rumble of Tom's truck. She hurried to open the door for him before he had a chance to ring the doorbell, knowing the dog would bark and the boys would be out of bed again. Eve felt awkward facing Tom as he walked up to the door. He seemed ill at ease, too.

"Hello, Tom."

"Hi."

"Audrey is out on a date with Alan, and—"

"I know. Get your coat and come outside with me for a few minutes. Please?" He waited on the front step, his hands in his coat pockets, as she went inside to put on her coat and boots. The winter night was beautiful, the air so crisp and clear that Eve could see millions of stars sparkling in the sky. If they drove out to Tom's farm in the country, away from the village lights, she knew that millions more stars would be visible, along with the great white swath of the Milky Way. She loved gazing up into the country sky at night.

"What brings you into town?"

"I came to give you your Christmas gift." He pulled an unwrapped box from his pocket and handed it to her. It was an ordinary white box, the kind that a necklace or a pair of earrings might have come in. She opened it and saw a diamond ring in a gold-filigree setting nestled on the cotton batting. It looked like an antique. "The ring belonged to my grandmother," Tom said. "I'm asking you to marry me."

Joy and panic wrestled with each other in Eve's heart. She wanted to say yes, yet she couldn't say yes.

She needed to hold Tom in her arms, yet she needed to push him away. She was afraid to love him, yet afraid that if she didn't, she would lose him. She stared down at the ring, not at him.

"If you accept this ring, Eve, and agree to set a date for the wedding, that will be your Christmas gift to me. If not, then I need to stop hoping. I need to stop caring. I want to marry you and adopt Harry as my son and raise a family with you. I want my farm to belong to you and Harry and to be the place where we work together and spend all of our Christmases together like my parents and grandparents did."

She looked up, staring into the distance, not at Tom. The colored Christmas tree lights in her neighbors' windows blurred as her eyes filled with tears. She had never met her daddy, who had died in the Great War before Eve was born. But from what everyone had told her about him, he was a kind, gentle man like Tom who had loved farming the land and tending his animals. Eve's granny used to say that Eve had inherited her love of the woods from him. To have a home and a future with Tom was everything she could have wished for. If only . . .

"I can't wait any longer to marry you, Eve. If you

accept this ring, then I want to set a date for our wedding. One that's only months from now, not years."

"I have to work to pay back—"

"If you were my wife, we could work together. You could pay back your debt faster if you weren't also paying rent."

"But part of the reason I need to pay Audrey back is to prove that I'm sorry."

"She knows you're sorry. Do you think she would have asked you to live in this house with her if she hadn't forgiven you?"

"I need to prove that I've changed. That I'm trying to be a better person, and—"

Tom took her shoulders in his hands, gripping them tightly. "I don't know who you see when you look in the mirror, Eve, but you need to start seeing what God sees—a woman who is worthy of a second chance." He pulled her close and held her tightly. Eve's heart was beating so hard that it hurt to breathe. "I'm tired of waiting, Eve. You can let me know your answer on Christmas Day when I come to the birthday party." He released her and walked to his truck.

Eve went inside and hung up her coat. Then she sank onto the couch with her face in her hands and wept.

* * *

Eve was still awake, sitting in the darkened living room with only the Christmas tree lights for illumination, when Audrey returned home after midnight. She saw the lights from Alan's car pull into the driveway, but a few minutes passed before Audrey came inside. "Did you and Alan have a good time?" Eve asked her when she did.

"Yes. A very lovely time."

Eve remembered the dreamy look Audrey had worn when she'd fallen in love with Robert, and although that same look wasn't there yet, Audrey did seem contented.

"Did you stay up late just so you could interrogate me about my date?" she asked with a smile.

"Not exactly. I *am* curious to hear how it went, but I also need to talk to you about something else."

Audrey took off her coat and kicked off her shoes before sinking down on a chair with a sigh, her crinoline rustling. Eve was barely listening as Audrey talked about the dinner and the dancing afterwards and admitted that she'd enjoyed Alan's company a lot. "But Alan and I have both decided that we are simply good friends, for now."

"Isn't that what I said before you left?"

"It is. And he also thanked us again for letting him be part of all our activities this Christmas. I didn't tell him that it was all your doing and that I gave you a hard time about it." She sighed again, then said, "What's in the box?" Eve was still holding it in her hands with the lid closed as if it contained something dangerous. Perhaps it did.

"Tom came here earlier tonight. He gave me this Christmas present." Eve opened the lid and held the box out to show Audrey the ring. "He asked me to marry him."

A huge smile spread across Audrey's face as if she was about to offer her congratulations. Then her smile faded. "Why isn't the ring on your finger?"

Eve closed the lid. "I don't know if I can accept it."

"But you love him."

"I do, but I have . . . obligations."

"Not to me. Eve, please don't feel that you owe me anything. You don't."

"Tom was my best friend before you came. But he's such a good man, Audrey, and I'm not a good person. I have an illegitimate son. Fathered by a married man, no less."

"You asked God to forgive you, remember? And you know that He has. That's what Christmas is all about. It's why He sent Jesus, isn't it? So we could be forgiven. And Tom knows the truth as well."

"Yes, I know I'm forgiven. But my sins still have consequences. I stole from you when I impersonated you for four years. I lived in a house that wasn't mine, spent money that was yours, drove your car all around. I owe you, Audrey, and I intend to pay you back."

"And I've told you again and again that you don't owe me anything. The only reason I agreed to accept your rent money, and the other payments you insist on giving me, is because I hoped it would bring you healing from your past."

"If nothing else, I need to keep working and helping you out so you can fulfill your dream of becoming a nurse. I need to be here for the next two years so you can go to college."

"I'm grateful, Eve. Bobby and I would have been lost without your help. But I've been doing a lot of thinking lately, and I've decided that maybe I'm too dependent on you. Maybe it's time I started getting by on my own."

"Yes, but after you finish nursing school, right?"

Audrey didn't seem to hear her. "All this time I've been trying to prove to myself—and to Robert—that I didn't need to rely on his parents' support or their wealth. Prove that I was able to pursue a nursing career and get by on my own."

"That's what you wanted, isn't it?"

"It is. And yet I'm leaning on you for support, Eve. It was wonderful of you to help Bobby and me get settled, but . . . well . . . we're settled. You and I both need to get on with our lives. It's time. From now on, I'm not taking any more rent money from you."

"You're just saying that so I'll accept Tom's proposal. But how can I marry him if I still haven't made up for all my mistakes?"

"You aren't the only person who has made mistakes. I should have come to America right after the war, when you came. I shouldn't have allowed fear to hold me back. If I had, then you wouldn't owe me any money."

"I was wrong to steal your identity."

"That's another mistake that was just as much mine as yours. I should have helped you, Eve. Instead, I was so mired in my own grief that I didn't see that you had no place to go and no way to support yourself and

Harry. I let you walk away without helping you. You're my dearest friend, and I let you down."

"I don't see it that way."

"Tom loves you and you love him. Accept his proposal. Live happily ever after."

"But what about your nursing degree?"

"I steered a boat into a war zone through rough seas, remember? I'm perfectly capable of steering Bobby and myself through choppy waters. As for my nursing degree, Robert's father offered to pay for all of it—as a gift. I wouldn't even have to mortgage this house. But instead of graciously accepting his gift, I've been stubbornly trying to prove something to Robert—who isn't even here! I've been trying to prove to him that I could get by on my own without any assistance from his parents. And all the while, I've been accepting money and support from you. Maybe it's time I swallowed my pride and let Robert's parents help me."

"You need to sleep on this, Audrey—"

"And you need to accept Tom's proposal. If you love him, and I know you do, put his ring on your finger and give Harry a daddy for Christmas."

Eve longed to do it, but she was afraid. She couldn't shake the notion that she hadn't paid her debt yet and that she didn't deserve to be happy until she did. How could she saddle Tom with such a burden?

"Come on," Audrey said. Her crinoline rustled again as she pulled herself to her feet. "Let's go to bed." She scooped up her shoes and carried them toward the hallway while Eve unplugged the Christmas tree lights. As if by silent agreement, they peeked into the boys' bedroom to check on them one last time. Harry and Bobby were both asleep on Cooper's rug on the floor with the dog cuddled between them. Cooper lifted his head and looked at them. Eve could have sworn he was grinning.

"Well, I did tell them not to let the dog get into bed with them," Eve said. She lifted Harry in her arms and kissed his forehead before tucking him in to the top bunk. Audrey moved Bobby into his bed on the bottom. Cooper turned in a circle and pawed at his rug a few times before settling back down to sleep.

"We can't think only about ourselves, Eve," Audrey said as they got ready for bed. "We owe our sons a life that's free from all the mistakes and griefs of our own past."

"That's what I'm trying to do by paying you back. How else can I start all over again?"

Audrey didn't reply.

Eve looked at Tom's ring again before setting the box on the dresser for the night. She turned off the light and climbed into bed. Was Audrey serious about wanting to live here on her own and not letting Eve help her? How could she raise Bobby and go to school at the same time? Eve didn't know where Audrey had gotten the courage to make all of these decisions, but surely she would see things differently in the morning. She would realize how much she still needed Eve's help. Eve closed her eyes, trying to picture herself as Tom's wife, living on the farm in the country with him, sleeping beside him at night, hearing Harry calling Tom "Daddy." It was easy to do. It was what she wanted more than anything else. And yet . . .

* * *

Eve had slept poorly. She was glad it was Saturday and she didn't have to go to work. After eating breakfast and taking Cooper for his walk, they all decided it was time for the little Wise Men to go shopping.

"Tomorrow is Sunday, and Monday is Christmas Eve, so this is our last chance," Audrey told the boys.

"How many presents do we need for everybody who's coming?" Harry asked.

Bobby counted off the names on his fingers. "There's Nana, Granddad, Grandma and Grandpa Van, Uncle Tom, and Mr. Hamilton. Six presents. They're all coming, right, Mummy?"

"Yes, they're all coming," Audrey replied. And Eve would have to give Tom her answer on Christmas Day. She had only three days to decide.

Harry put his hands over Cooper's ears for a moment and whispered, "He needs a present, too."

Bobby held up another finger. "That makes seven presents." The boys dumped all of the money they had earned doing chores around the house onto the living room floor, and Audrey helped them count it. "Do we have enough, Mummy?"

"You have plenty." Eve looked at the collection of quarters and nickels and dimes and gave Audrey a worried look. Audrey simply smiled.

Eve's concern deepened when they arrived in town and Audrey headed to the department store first. The boys knew nothing about prices and were certain to choose expensive gifts. But they found a special display of reasonably priced Christmas gifts and chose

Old Spice cologne and shaving brush sets for Tom and his father, and a Yardley of London lavender-scented bubble bath and talcum powder set for Grandma Van.

It occurred to Eve that if she accepted Tom's proposal, she and Harry would be celebrating Christmas at the farm next year. But how could she leave Audrey and Bobby on their own? She sighed and trailed through the store aisles with the others while Bing Crosby and Perry Como crooned Christmas music in the background.

Finding something for Alan and the well-to-do Barretts was going to be more difficult. But Bobby remembered how much Nana liked to have photographs sitting everywhere, and they chose a nice, double picture frame that was just the right size for the Polaroid instant pictures of the boys from the Christmas party. Harry thought Granddad would like a set of pipe tools in a zippered pouch for the pipes he enjoyed smoking. That left Mr. Hamilton and Cooper.

"Mr. Hamilton needs a new whistle," Bobby said, "for when we play games at Boys' Club. He lost his."

"Yeah! One with a strap that goes around his neck," Harry said. Woolworth's had whistles and several different lanyards to choose from. The boys picked a bright-red one. "So he won't lose it again."

Last of all, they found a ball that they thought Cooper might enjoy chasing. The five-and-dime store also had wrapping paper and ribbons and tape.

"And balloons! We need balloons."

"And candles! How old is Jesus going to be, Mummy?"

Eve and Audrey both laughed. "Well, I'm not sure. More than a thousand years, I would think."

"We'll just light a whole bunch," Bobby decided.

Their last stop was Davidson's Bakery to order a birthday cake. The boys stood in front of the display case, drooling over the cookies and éclairs and pastries inside it and smearing the glass with their mitten-prints.

"We'd like to order a birthday cake for eleven people," Audrey told Mrs. Davidson. She was a motherly woman, as plump and jolly and white-haired as Mrs. Santa Claus.

"Eleven people?" Eve asked. "Are you counting Cooper?"

"Of course," Audrey laughed.

"Your cake will be ready for pickup on Christmas Eve," Mrs. Davidson said. "Come any time between ten and noon."

"Can you write *Happy Birthday* on it?" Harry asked.

"Certainly." The woman smiled down at him from over the counter. "Which one of you boys is having a birthday?"

Harry started to giggle. "It's not for us. It's for Jesus." She gave him a blank look. "Christmas is Jesus' birthday and He needs a birthday cake."

"It needs to say *Happy Birthday, Jesus,*" Bobby added.

"Oh, now I understand!" she said with a laugh. "Of course!"

"We're gonna have a party with cake and ice cream and presents and everything," Harry said.

The woman smiled as she wrote out their order on her pad. "You know, in all the years that my husband and I have owned this bakery, this is the very first time that anyone has ever bought a birthday cake for Jesus. I think it's a wonderful idea."

The boys opened their shopping bags and spread out all of the gifts they'd purchased on the dining room table when they returned home. Eve and Audrey taught them how to wrap presents and helped them do it themselves. "Let's put them beneath the tree until the party," Bobby said. Afterwards, they put on their coats and galoshes and went outside to play in the snow with Cooper.

"I'm so proud of our boys, aren't you?" Audrey asked

as they cleared all the scraps and wrapping supplies from the table. "They had fun picking out the presents themselves. And you should have seen them working around here like Christmas elves all week to earn the money." She looked up at Eve and said, "What? What's wrong?"

Eve hadn't realized that her mood was so obvious. She decided to tell Audrey the truth. "It looks so bare under the tree."

"Well, of course. Santa Claus hasn't come yet."

"If only the Wish Book hadn't filled them with grand ideas for all the toys Santa is going to bring. I know we bought a few presents, but I'm so afraid Harry will be disappointed."

"Yet if we had bought them everything they wanted, what would happen next year—and the year after that? It would only build up their expectations for more and more every year."

"I wish they'd never seen that silly Wish Book," Eve grumbled.

"But think about how far they've come since that first day. Giving their Wise Men gifts really has taught them something. They've been so excited about earning money and picking out presents for people. There may not be many presents under the tree, but the lessons they've learned have been priceless."

"We've been given gifts this Christmas, too," Eve said softly. "Alan's friendship has been a gift to you, hasn't it?"

"Yes. And you received a priceless gift from Tom. Are you going to accept his proposal?"

The question irritated her. "I don't know. Have you decided if you're going to accept Granddad Barrett's gift of a nursing degree?"

Audrey looked away. "I-I don't know."

"Then it looks like we both have some more thinking to do."

Chapter 12

Tomorrow was Christmas. Audrey watched Eve flip pancakes on the griddle and silently consulted a mental checklist of Christmas preparations, wondering if she had forgotten anything. The presents from Santa Claus were all wrapped and hidden away. The invitations to the birthday party had been sent, and everyone other than Mrs. Herder was planning to come. Even Alan Hamilton, which had surprised Audrey—and pleased her. "Let's see . . . ," she mused aloud. "We remembered to buy candles, the ice cream is in the freezer . . . and speaking of ice cream, I scrubbed all the chocolate stains from the boys' Sunday clothes after the party at the country club, but we'll need to iron their shirts before the Christmas Eve service tonight."

"Let's not forget to pick up the cake today."

"Right." Audrey longed to make Christmas a wonderful day for Bobby, but she worried, as Eve had last night, that he would be disappointed.

"What are you so worried about now?" Eve asked as if reading her mind.

"What makes you think I'm worried?"

"You're wearing that look you have whenever you fret. You have that line between your eyebrows, and your eyes are all squinty."

"They are not." She gave Eve a playful punch. "I'm just wondering if I've forgotten anything."

"Well, if you have, you'd better remember it soon. The stores all close early on Christmas Eve."

"I'm so glad you have today off," Audrey said, "so we can enjoy it together."

"I am, too. Call the boys. The pancakes are done. I made a lot, so I hope they aren't too excited to eat them."

Harry was very excited and couldn't seem to sit still

as they gathered around the kitchen table for breakfast. "Santa Claus is coming tonight, right, Mommy?" he asked with a mouthful of pancakes.

"Yes. But please don't talk with your mouth full," Eve told him.

"Do we have enough cookies for Santa?" Bobby asked. Audrey had forgotten about the tradition of leaving a plate of cookies for Santa Claus and some carrots for his reindeer. They weren't on her checklist.

"I think there are a few cookies left." She stood and lifted the cookie jar from the counter to check when the telephone in the hallway rang. She went to answer it, carrying the jar with her.

"Audrey, it's me. Do you have a minute?" She recognized her father-in-law's somber voice and immediately began to worry. He never telephoned her.

"Yes, of course. Is everything all right?"

"We're fine, fine. Listen, I know it's Christmas Eve, and you probably have a lot of things going on today, but . . . well, our law firm received some documents that I need to talk over with you."

Audrey wanted to scold him for working on Christmas Eve and ask if it couldn't have waited two more days, but she didn't dare.

"My associate brought them to my attention the other day. They're from your father's solicitor in England."

Audrey sank down on the seat on the telephone stand with the cookie jar on her lap. Her *father*? "How did his lawyer even find me—and your law firm?"

"They were directed here by your uncle in London." That made sense. Audrey had corresponded with her aunt and uncle, letting them know that she and Bobby were well and getting on in America.

"What sort of documents are they?"

"I think it would be simpler if you came over so I could explain everything to you in person. I'm working from home today. I don't think you'll want to wait until after Christmas." Robert had complained that his father often put his work before his family. The fact that he was working on Christmas Eve reminded Audrey of why Robert hadn't wanted to join his father's law firm. "Have Eve come as well," Mr. Barrett added. "My wife can watch the boys for you."

"We're just finishing breakfast, and then we'll need to walk our neighbor's dog, but we'll be there shortly." She hung up the receiver and went back to the kitchen. "Well, that was very mysterious. Mr. Barrett wants me to come over to the house. He says he received some documents from my father's lawyer in London."

"Is it good news or bad news?" Eve asked.

"He didn't say. But he wants you to come, too."

"Me? What for?"

"I don't know. Maybe it's something so terrible that he knows I'll fall apart and I'll need you to hold me together."

Eve shook her head. "Audrey the worrier."

"You must admit it all sounds very intriguing—important documents on Christmas Eve?"

Bobby tugged on her apron. "Do we have enough cookies, Mummy?"

"Pardon?"

"For Santa. He's coming tonight and he'll be hungry."

Audrey realized she was still holding the jar. She lifted the lid and peered inside. "There should be enough, provided you boys stay away from them." She glanced at Eve. "I can't imagine what kind of documents they could be."

*　*　*

The boys ran off to visit with Nana as soon as they arrived at the Barretts' home, and Mr. Barrett led Audrey and Eve into his mahogany-paneled study. He took a seat behind his massive desk and motioned for them to take the two chairs in front of it. The formality added to Audrey's sense of dread. "First of all, Audrey, I want to say how very sorry I am about the loss of your father."

His words stole her breath. "What? He *died*?" She had told herself that she no longer cared about Alfred Clarkson after the cruel way he'd treated her, selling her beloved home, Wellingford Hall, and leaving her and Bobby virtually penniless. But the breathless grief she suddenly felt for him told her that she'd been mistaken. She did care for the man she'd grown up believing was her father. "I-I didn't know he had died."

"I'm so sorry, Audrey. I was certain you would have heard. I wouldn't have sprung the news on you this way otherwise."

"We weren't in touch at all. Shortly before I left England, he put our home up for sale and disinherited me."

"Disinherited you?"

"This is embarrassing, but . . . when Alfred Clarkson told me he wasn't my real father, he made it clear that I didn't have any right to his home or his money."

"I see. Well, according to these documents, his lawyers in Britain have been going over his will to settle his estate, and it seems that he did leave you a bequest after all."

"A bequest?"

"Yes, a gift."

Audrey sat forward in her chair. It was unimaginable that he would do that.

"Mr. Clarkson specifically asked that it be designated as a gift. It's quite a large sum of money, in fact. I've calculated the dollar amount according to today's exchange rate." He passed a paper across the desk to her. Audrey stared in disbelief.

"That's . . . that's over a hundred thousand dollars!"

Eve peered at it too and whistled. "Didn't I always say he was richer than King George?"

Audrey tried to speak but nothing came out.

"There's more," Mr. Barrett said, passing her a second piece of paper. "This is a copy of the deed to a town house in London that now belongs to you."

"That can't be right." Audrey shook her head as if to dislodge her confusion. "The town house was destroyed during the Blitz."

"According to these documents, Mr. Clarkson had it rebuilt. And since the original deed to the property was in your mother's name, he said the town house right-fully belongs to you. The lawyers are asking what you would like them to do with it."

Audrey leaned back in her chair, holding her fore-head as the room seemed to spin. She must be dream-ing. None of this could be true.

"Are you all right?" Eve asked. "You look a little faint."

"I feel faint! This is such a shock! Why . . . why couldn't he have given me all this news a year and a half ago? Before I uprooted my life and moved across the ocean?"

"It seems that your father—I mean Mr. Clarkson—decided to revise his will only recently, shortly before he died. Nearly all of his assets will go to various charities, but he specifically earmarked this gift for you and your son. And he included this letter."

Tears filled Audrey's eyes as she took the sealed enve-lope from Mr. Barrett and tore it open. Her father never had seemed to care about her and had certainly never shown her any love. But to remember her now . . . on his deathbed? Perhaps he had cared after all. She pulled the letter from the envelope.

Dear Audrey,

I am a dying man with many regrets, and chief among them is the way I treated you and your son. I allowed bitterness and grief to poison me after Alfie and your mother died, and you didn't deserve to be treated so shamefully. As I now prepare to face my Maker, I pray you will find it in your heart to forgive me. You were a kind and loyal daughter to me in spite of my failings as a father.

The gift I've designated for you in my will is not an attempt to buy your forgiveness but is given because you are my daughter, joined to me by the family we loved and shared. I am sorry that it will come too late for us to be reconciled, but my wish for you and your son is that you will have a happy life, surrounded by people you love.

Sincerely,
Alfred Clarkson

When she finished, Audrey refolded the letter and tucked it back into the envelope.

"What does it say?" Eve asked.

"He . . ." She cleared the lump from her throat.

"He asked me to forgive him. He called me his . . . his daughter."

"Oh, Audrey," Eve breathed. "I'm so happy for you. All these years, you thought—"

"I know. I thought he didn't care about Bobby and me. But maybe he did." She looked up at her father-in-law again, at a loss for words.

"It will take time for Mr. Clarkson's lawyers to sell off all of his businesses and stocks and other assets in order to settle the estate," Mr. Barrett said. "In the meantime, they'll need to know whether to wire the money here or to an account in London. The town house is available for you to move into if you wish, and your bequest can be set up as an annuity that will provide you with an income. Although I certainly hope you will continue to feel that this is your home."

"You're rich, Audrey!" Eve grabbed her hand, squeezing it. "You can move back home to London if you want."

Audrey could only shake her head and mumble, "I can't . . . I can't comprehend this."

"You're mentioned in Mr. Clarkson's will as well, Eve."

"Me?" She gave a little laugh. "That can't be right. Are you sure?"

"The will states that a gift should also be given to the family of Mrs. Clarkson's longtime lady's maid, Mrs. Ellen Dawson, for her loyalty to Mrs. Clarkson on the night she died."

"What?" Eve clutched Audrey's arm.

"Am I correct in assuming that Ellen Dawson was your mother?"

Eve nodded. She looked as stunned as Audrey felt. "Our mothers died together when a bomb struck our London town house," Audrey explained.

"Your gift, Eve, with the current exchange rate, is just over twelve thousand dollars."

Eve threw her arms around Audrey, hugging her tightly. "I can pay you back, Audrey!" she wept. "I can pay back all the money I spent."

Audrey pried Eve's arms away, laughing through her own tears. "Eve, look at this!" she said, shoving her paper into Eve's hands. "I don't need any more money. I told you from the beginning that you didn't have to pay me back, but you were so bullheaded about it."

"But it was wrong of me to steal your name and pretend to be you. Your family is wealthy and belongs to the aristocracy, and I'm just their scullery maid. I'm nobody—"

"Don't say that!" Audrey said fiercely. "Do you think God looks at our wealth and social class to decide who's worthy of His love? Every person is valuable in His sight. And every job we do in His name is valuable. I think that's what my father was trying to say when he gave this gift to your mother's family. Ellen served as Mother's lady's maid unselfishly and with all her heart." Audrey turned to her father-in-law again. He wore a rare smile, as if pleased to have given them such wonderful news on Christmas Eve. "I can't comprehend this," she said. "I don't think either of us can."

"You don't need to make any decisions today. I just wanted to let you know about these surprise Christmas gifts. I thought it would brighten your holidays."

Audrey left the study arm in arm with Eve. "You can return home to London, Audrey," Eve said again. "You'll have a home and an income there."

"You could come with me. The town house is twice the size of our bungalow. We could easily live in it together." Home. She and Eve and Bobby and Harry could go home to England.

Eve was still shaking her head. "I can't believe that your father would give me this . . . this gift. I didn't do anything to deserve it."

"I did nothing to deserve my gift, either. It's . . . it's amazing." They were still clinging to each other when they reached the living room. The boys were sitting on the floor near the Christmas tree, playing with the electric train set while Nana watched. They barely looked up when their mothers entered.

"I'm taking turns," Harry announced.

"Me, too," Bobby echoed.

"Would you mind watching the boys for an hour or so?" Eve asked Mrs. Barrett. "Audrey and I need to run a quick errand."

Audrey had no idea what errand Eve was talking about. She was about to protest but Nana said, "Of course not. Take your time."

Eve pulled Audrey toward the door and retrieved their coats from the closet.

"Are we picking up the cake?" Audrey asked. "I think the boys would like to come along with us for that."

"We can get the cake later."

"Well, what's going on, then? Where are we going? I can't take any more surprises today."

"You'll see," Eve replied. She hurried Audrey to the car.

"Well, wherever we're going, you'd better drive,"

Audrey said as she went to the passenger side. "I'm not sure I can or should be behind the wheel. I'm still in shock."

"I know how you feel." Eve started the engine and drove the few miles from the Barretts' elegant neighborhood to the village center. The town was bustling with activity on Christmas Eve, and they searched for several minutes for a parking space.

"Tell me what we're doing here, Eve," she said as they got out of the car. Audrey was a little afraid that it had something to do with Alan, since Eve was always pushing him into her life.

"We're going to buy those aluminum airplanes that Harry and Bobby want so badly."

"Are you serious?" Audrey pulled Eve to a stop in the middle of the sidewalk, forcing the other pedestrians to weave around them. "I thought we'd decided not to indulge their greed by buying them too many toys."

"It's Christmas, Audrey!" Eve looked happy enough to float into the air like a helium balloon.

"I know that, but—"

"Harry and Bobby both love that airplane. And now we can both afford to buy them one!"

"Well, I know, but even so—"

"Listen, if Robert were here, don't you think he would buy that shiny new airplane for Bobby? Maybe a dozen airplanes!"

Tears filled Audrey's eyes as she pictured Robert strolling through the toy department, grinning as he picked out gifts for their son. It would have brought him joy. Audrey's father had just shown his love for her by giving her an extravagant gift. And it reminded Audrey that her heavenly Father had shown His extravagant love by giving Jesus to the world at Christmas.

"You're right," she said, wiping her eyes. "Robert would have bought every toy in the Wish Book. And besides, I'm no longer spending Bobby's trust fund money. This is my very own money."

"I know! For the first time in my life I have money of my own. I can splurge on anything I want. I feel like a weight has been lifted off my shoulders, Audrey."

They hurried to the store together and bought two aluminum airplanes, asking the clerk to gift wrap them. As she left the store with her gift, Audrey couldn't remember ever having so much fun spending money.

Chapter 13

THE CHURCH WAS PACKED that evening for the Christmas Eve candlelight service. Eve crammed into a pew beside Audrey and their two boys to hear the story of Jesus' birth retold and to sing all the old familiar carols. The scent of fresh pine permeated the sanctuary, filling Eve with longing for the woods. The day had flown by since she'd learned about Mr. Clarkson's gift this morning. She couldn't have said what she'd done after retrieving the boys from the Barretts' house and picking up the cake and buying more cookies from the bakery. All she had been able to think about was this life-changing gift. It was unexpected, undeserved, unbelievable. She was still trying to comprehend it when the pastor began his Christmas Eve message.

"This evening, I want us to join the Wise Men, who traveled from the East to bring their gifts to Jesus."

Harry had been wiggling beside Eve, but he froze at the minister's words and whispered, "Mommy! The Wise Men!" Eve nodded and put her finger to her lips.

"Guided by a star, they 'fell down, and worshipped him: and when they had opened their treasures, they presented unto him gifts; gold, and frankincense, and myrrh.' These were gifts for a king in a palace, not a poor infant in a stable. They brought Him gold—gold for the One who created the universe and its infinite stars. Gold for the One who said 'the world is mine, and the fulness thereof'; 'every beast of the forest is mine, and the cattle upon a thousand hills.' How foolish we are to think we can give anything back to God. We can't earn His grace and favor by our own efforts. No amount of money or gold or good deeds can pay for forgiveness."

That's what she had been trying to do, Eve realized. She'd been working hard and trying to repay Audrey in order to make up for all the wrong choices and mistakes she had made. *How foolish.* The words seemed meant for her alone.

"We each owe a debt that we can never repay. But God has reached down from heaven to pay it for us, giving us the gift of Jesus. He offers His forgiveness to us as a gift, to show 'the exceeding riches of his grace . . . For by grace are ye saved through faith; and that not of yourselves: it is the gift of God: not of works, lest any man should boast.' God delights in giving this gift to us, the way we delight in giving gifts to our children."

The word *gift* echoed in Eve's heart. She had delighted in buying the airplane for Harry. And thanks to Audrey's father, she'd seen what a true gift was— something she'd done nothing to deserve, given to her only because of the wealth and generosity of the giver. She could do nothing in return for the Savior who had freely forgiven her.

"The Wise Men brought frankincense and myrrh to Jesus," the pastor continued, "expensive gifts that were used to bring healing, to soothe pain, and to anoint the dead for burial. They gave frankincense and myrrh to the One who 'hath borne our griefs, and carried our sorrows,' the One who 'was wounded for our trans- gressions . . . bruised for our iniquities . . . and with his stripes we are healed.' This became the greatest gift exchange of all time—we bring to Christ our sorrow and grief. We bring our sin and shame and lay them at His feet. And in return, He gives us comfort and forgiveness and everlasting life with our heavenly Father."

Eve bowed her head as her tears overflowed. She had asked God for forgiveness, and she knew that He had given it. Why, then, had she been trying to repay a debt that had already been paid? Everyone had forgiven her—Audrey, the Barretts, Tom and his parents. But she had refused to forgive herself.

"Myrrh was brought to Jesus at His birth, and again after His death on the cross, because even as the innocent Christ child lay in His manger in a stable, His death on a cross for you and for me had already been planned by God since the creation of the world. Like the Wise Men who witnessed His coming and bowed to worship Him, we are walking witnesses to His grace, showing His saving power to the world. That is what God's gift at Christmas accomplishes. The weight of our guilt and sin has been lifted from our shoulders. And what does He ask of us in return? 'To do justly, and to love mercy, and to walk humbly with thy God.'"

Eve pulled a handkerchief from her pocket to wipe

her tears, remembering Tom telling her she was worthy of a second chance. She had felt the weight of her debt to Audrey being lifted from her shoulders when she'd learned of Mr. Clarkson's gift. And now she was reminded that an even greater debt had been lifted. Tears of joy closed Eve's throat. She was too emotional to sing the closing hymn, "Silent Night." Audrey looked deeply moved as well. They hugged each other without speaking as the candlelight service quietly ended.

Eve still felt dazed as they drove home and helped Harry and Bobby get ready for bed. Audrey made hot chocolate, and they brought it into the living room with a plate of cookies from the bakery to have a little party beside the Christmas tree. And as Eve delighted in her son's squirming happiness and his anticipation of what tomorrow would bring, Eve knew that the fierce and tender love she had for her son was just a fraction of what her heavenly Father felt for her.

The boys set out a plate of cookies for Santa Claus and some carrots for his reindeer. Audrey read them a story to help them settle down before bed, but Harry was still wiggling and giggling when she finished.

"I'm so excited!" he said.

"Me, too! Me, too!" Bobby said.

"Because Santa Claus is coming tonight?" Eve asked.

"Yeah, and because of the birthday party tomorrow! Wait until you see what we—"

"Don't tell!" Bobby shouted so loudly that Cooper barked.

Everyone laughed as Harry put his hand over his mouth. Audrey had told Eve about the friendly wager between Tom and Alan, guessing which boy would be the first to give away their secret. Eve expected it to be Harry. Twice now, he nearly had given it away before Bobby stopped him. The boys hung their stockings on their bedposts, and they all said good night with kisses and hugs. Audrey agreed to let Cooper stay in the boys' room for a while.

Afterwards, Eve and Audrey went into the living room together, but neither of them felt like turning on the television. Audrey put a Christmas album on the phonograph instead, turning the volume down low.

"I think that sermon was meant just for me," Eve said.

"No, it was also meant for me. I realized that I've been hanging on to my sorrow and grief for Robert instead of offering it to God and allowing Him to heal it. Even Robert's mother must have done that, or else she wouldn't have been able to wish for my happiness with Alan."

"You aren't being unfaithful to Robert or to your memories of him if you're happy. And if you love again."

"I see that, now. Mrs. Herder talked about making grief into a shrine, like the gold star that used to be in her window, and that's what I've done. Now I need to stop trying to live the life I think Robert would want me to live and live the one that God is giving me."

Eve smiled. "And it seems to me that God is determined to keep you rich."

"Yes," Audrey laughed. "It seems He is indeed!"

"You know, Robert was raised with wealth and he still made wise decisions. So did you, growing up. You could have chosen the things that Alfie did. Having money doesn't make you a bad person."

"It's like the pastor said in his sermon: God asks us to be just and merciful and to walk humbly with Him. Instead of trying to avoid wealth, I should probably ask for His help in managing it wisely—like maybe giving a nursing scholarship to a young woman who needs it."

"And I think I know a handsome young banker who would be happy to help you with advice about investments."

"Yes . . . Alan . . ." Audrey sighed. "Thank you for pushing him into our lives, Eve. I do enjoy his company."

Suddenly the dog came trotting out from the bedroom and gave a little bark. Seconds later, the doorbell rang. Eve tried to shush him before he barked again. "Shh! Quiet, Cooper. You'll wake up the boys." Audrey held on to his collar while Eve went to open the door. A woman she didn't know stood on the doorstep holding two large, wrapped presents. "Hello. This must be the right house because I recognize Cooper. Are you Eve or Audrey?"

"I'm Eve Dawson."

"I'm Clara Jackson, a friend of Mrs. Herder. She ordered these toys for your two boys from the Sears Wish Book and had them sent to my house. She asked me to deliver them to you on Christmas Eve and to tell your sons they're from Santa Claus."

"My goodness! Thank you." Eve took one of the packages from her, and Audrey let go of Cooper's collar to take the other.

Mrs. Jackson lowered her voice and said, "They're fire engines with ladders that move up and down. I peeked before I wrapped them up." Eve thanked the woman, who refused their offer to come inside for tea and cookies, and closed the door again.

"Dear, kind Mrs. Herder," Audrey murmured. "We'll need to write her a thank-you note."

"I think this is her thank-you note to us."

"I suppose you're right." They put the new gifts beneath the tree, then Eve tiptoed into the boys' bedroom to check on them. They were asleep.

"I think it's time for Santa Claus to come," she told Audrey when she came out again. They retrieved the first presents they had purchased from their hiding place in the bedroom closet and put them beneath the tree. The gift-wrapped airplanes she and Audrey had purchased that afternoon were still in the trunk of Audrey's car. They were about to put on their coats to bring the packages inside when Cooper gave another bark. The doorbell rang again.

"Shh!" Audrey said, holding his collar. Eve opened the door and was stunned to see her boss from work, holding a wrapped Christmas present.

"Mr. Carpenter! Hello! Would you like to come in?"

"No thank you. I have a few more errands to run tonight. This present is for you, Eve. I didn't have a chance to give it to you before the office closed for

Christmas, but I wanted to show my appreciation for all your hard work. You're always so cheerful and reliable and diligent. I don't thank you often enough for the fine work you do."

"Thank you," she managed to say. Seeing her boss made Eve realize again that she had been working all this time to repay a debt that had already been forgiven.

"The other typists told me how you and your friend are raising your sons on your own," Mr. Carpenter continued. "So I just wanted to say how much I admire you for that."

"Thank you . . . That's so kind of you . . ."

"Please accept this gift with my gratitude and in the spirit of the season. Merry Christmas, Eve."

She closed the door and leaned against it, still holding the present. "I don't think I can take any more surprise gifts today," she said. Audrey laughed and took the package from her, shaking it as she put it beneath the tree as if trying to judge what was inside. "I can't believe my boss brought me a gift."

"He honored you for the work you faithfully do, the same way my father honored your mother with a generous gift for her loyalty. And did you hear what he said about you, Eve? You're always so hard on yourself because of what you've done in the past, but no one else sees you as a terrible person. We all see the wonderful, hardworking woman we love."

Tom had tried to tell her the same thing. Maybe it was time she stopped punishing herself and accepted forgiveness. She drew a deep breath and let it out with a sigh. "Right. Now let's go get those presents from the car." They put on their coats and boots and fastened Cooper's leash to his collar to go outside. Afterwards, Eve stared at the growing pile of presents beneath the tree as she sank down on the sofa again. "Harry was right when he said we'd need to lop off some branches to make more room under the tree." She took one of the cookies the boys had set out for Santa and bit into it. "We still haven't talked about the surprise gifts from your father."

"I can't comprehend it, Eve. The town house . . . and enough income to live on? It doesn't seem real."

"Do you think you'll go back home to London?"

Audrey picked up a cookie, too, holding it for a moment. "I've been thinking about it all afternoon, and again in church tonight, trying to decide what to do. I might have gone back to London a year ago. But this is my home now. Bobby's home. All of our friends are here. And our family. We have all become a family, haven't we, Eve? You and me and Nana and Granddad Barrett and Tom and Grandma and Grandpa Van . . ."

"And don't forget Mrs. Herder and Cooper. And your new friend Alan."

Cooper had been asleep at Eve's feet, but he suddenly lifted his head and barked. Seconds later, the doorbell rang. "Not again!" Eve said, laughing. "I'll hold Cooper this time. You go answer it."

Audrey opened the door and said, "Alan!"

"Merry Christmas, Audrey." He was carrying two packages.

"Come in, come in! Merry Christmas. But you're early for the birthday party."

Alan laughed. "I know. Here, I brought these for Harry and Bobby. I liked your idea of giving away Wise Men gifts, so I decided to buy a present for each of my Boys' Club members. It's just some things the boys will need when they go to the church campout next year—a flashlight, canteen, compass, a mess kit. And there's a penknife in there, too. It isn't sharp. I hope you don't mind them having one."

"Not if you teach them how to use it properly."

"I will. But please tell them the gifts are from Santa, not me."

"That's very kind of you, Alan. Would you like to stay and have some coffee or tea? We have cookies."

"No thanks. I have a few more of these to deliver."

"Alan, look up," Eve called from across the room.

He did. "Is that mistletoe?" he asked with a grin.

"It is. I hung it there myself," Eve said. "I'll look away." But Eve peeked between her fingers as Alan gave Audrey a kiss.

"I'll see you at the birthday party tomorrow," he said.

Audrey closed the door and put Alan's presents beneath the tree with all the others. She was shaking her head. "Just look," she said. "Our boys gave away a few gifts, and look at all of the ones they received in return."

"Harry and Bobby aren't the only people who learned how much fun it is to be a Wise Man."

"What about you, Eve? What do you think you'll do with the gift from my father? I hope you believe me now when I tell you I don't need or want any of your money."

"I do believe you . . . finally. Tonight's sermon made me realize that I've been behaving like a child, trying to prove that I'm 'good' so I would deserve good gifts from Santa Claus. But God isn't Santa Claus. He's more like you and me, giving gifts to His children because

He loves us. I can't buy forgiveness or a new reputation, not by working hard, not even with all of the money your father gave me. Forgiveness is a free gift because of Christmas. He makes all things new."

"And so . . . you and Tom?"

"I think Tom and his family and the farm are all gifts to me from God. And I've been too ashamed and stubborn and stupid to accept them."

"We both had a lot to learn this Christmas about giving gifts, haven't we?"

Once again, the dog lifted his head and barked. Once again, the doorbell rang. Eve and Audrey burst into laughter. "Who could it possibly be this time?" Eve asked as she went to answer it.

"Maybe it's the real Santa Claus. We don't have a chimney, you know. He would have to ring the doorbell, wouldn't he?"

Eve opened the door—and there stood Tom! He was holding two long, narrow boxes, wrapped in Christmas paper. "I think Santa Claus dropped these off at my house by mistake," he said. "They're toy rifles. Every cowboy needs a rifle. They shoot corks, but I'll be happy to teach the boys how to shoot a BB gun when they're older. In the meantime, they still need to know

how to handle a gun and to never point it at anyone."
Eve looked up at him, unable to speak. "Eve? Why are
you crying?"

"Because . . . Harry is going to get another gift from
his Wish Book list—a daddy!"

"Does that mean . . . ?"

"Yes! It means I'm saying yes! Merry Christmas,
Tom!"

He dropped the presents and pulled her into his
arms.

Chapter 14

"Mummy! Mummy, wake up! It's Christmas!" Audrey opened her eyes to find Bobby standing beside her bed, shaking her. "Santa Claus came, Mummy! Wake up!"

Harry had climbed onto his mother's twin bed and was bouncing to awaken Eve. "You should see all of the presents under our tree, Mommy! Santa's sleigh must have been very full last night!"

"Did you go into the living room already?" Eve asked, her voice groggy.

"We peeked just a little," Harry replied. "Cooper wanted to see if Santa came, and he did, Mommy! He

247

did! He even ate our cookies and fed the carrots to his reindeer."

"It's barely light outside," Eve said, groaning. "What time is it?"

Audrey smiled as she looked at her alarm clock. "Twenty minutes until seven. But we may as well get up, Eve. You know none of us is going back to sleep." Audrey got out of bed and put on her dressing gown while Harry continued to bounce on his mother's bed.

"Wait until you see how many presents Santa brought, Mommy! And my name is on a lot of them!"

"I thought you just took a *little* peek," she said. But Eve was smiling and putting on her robe, too.

What followed was an explosion of ribbon and wrapping paper and hoots of delight as the boys ripped into their presents. "Wow! Look at this! This is just what I wanted!" they said over and over again. Audrey used the camera she'd purchased a few months ago to try to capture the expressions of astonishment and joy on Bobby's and Harry's faces. She was especially pleased by their reactions when they saw the shiny aluminum airplanes. "Santa remembered!" Bobby said. "He remembered!" He hugged the airplane to his chest.

When the last present had finally been opened,

Bobby and Harry sat on the floor like little kings, surrounded by their plunder. They seemed unable to decide which toy to play with first. "This is the best Christmas in my whole life!" Bobby said.

"Mine, too," Audrey said softly. And it was, if for no other reason than to see her son's joy. *This must be how our heavenly Father feels,* she thought, *when He gives good gifts to His children.* And Audrey was ready at last to accept His gifts.

"Our toy box is going to be so full!" Harry said.

Bobby tugged on Harry's pajama sleeve. "Maybe we can give some of them to other kids again, to make room."

"Yeah! Mommy, can we still give Wise Men presents *after* Christmas?"

"Of course," Eve said. "I think that's a wonderful idea."

Audrey leaned close to Eve and whispered, "They're getting it, Eve! Isn't it amazing?"

* * *

When it was time for the birthday party that afternoon, Harry and Bobby helped blow up the balloons and set the dining room table. The boys put the presents they had purchased for their party guests at each of their places. Audrey was surprised when Alan was the first to arrive, shortly before three. "I came to see if I could help with anything," he said. But the boys began tugging on his hands before he even had a chance to take off his coat.

"Look, Mr. Hamilton! Santa Claus brought us everything we need for the Boys' Club campout," Harry said.

"There's even a real pocketknife!" Bobby added. Alan grinned as he tried to look suitably surprised and amazed by the new gear that he had purchased.

A few minutes later, Tom's truck pulled into the driveway. Eve had been watching for him, and she raced outside without her coat to greet him. Audrey had tears in her eyes as she watched Eve run into his arms. Tom held her close, rocking her. Then Grandma and Grandpa Van got out of the car, and Eve hugged them, too. Audrey saw them laughing and wiping their tears. They all came inside and the boys opened their presents from Tom and his parents—two brand-new sleds.

"Now we can each ride on one," Bobby said.

"Yeah! We can have a race!"

"Santa Claus brought us the rifles we wanted, Uncle Tom."

"Will you teach us how to shoot them?"

"I'll be happy to." He ruffled Harry's red hair. Tom had also brought the two wrapped presents that the boys had purchased on their secret errand with him and Alan.

"They're for you and for Harry's mommy," Bobby told Audrey. "That's what our secret surprise was."

"Open yours now, Mommy! Open it now!" Harry begged.

"Shall I?" Eve asked.

"Yes! Wait till you see what I bought! We worked and worked out at the farm to earn all the money, and then I picked it out for you myself!"

"Open yours, too, Mummy," Bobby told Audrey as Eve began ripping the paper off her present. Audrey peeled the paper from hers carefully, as if she might want to reuse it, but she really just wanted to savor this tender moment. She glanced at Eve and saw that Harry had bought her a necklace with a heart-shaped locket.

"It opens up, Mommy, and you can put my picture in it."

"That's exactly what I'll do. It's beautiful, Harry. I love it," she said, hugging him.

"There's room for two pictures inside, if you want."

Eve looked at Tom as she fastened the locket around her neck. "I think I know whose picture that will be, too."

Audrey finished opening her present from Bobby, surprised to find a lovely gold compact with flowers engraved on the cover and a mirror inside. "Oh, my! It's gorgeous, Bobby. Thank you." She pulled him into her arms and kissed his forehead.

"You can keep it in your purse for when you want to put on your lipstick. Mr. Hamilton helped me pick it out."

"You both did a wonderful job," she said, looking at Alan. "I will treasure this."

"You mean, like pirate treasure?"

"Yes," Audrey said, laughing. "Like pirate treasure."

"Okay, it's time to settle my bet with Alan," Tom said. "Which one of the boys squealed first?"

"And how long were they able to keep it a secret?" Alan added.

"There were a few close calls," Audrey said. "But you'll be surprised to learn that neither one of them gave anything away."

Alan laughed. "I guess we both lose—or win, depending on how you look at it."

Nana and Granddad Barrett arrived last, their arms filled with more presents. Nana seemed very surprised when Cooper greeted her at the door. "My goodness! Did Santa Claus really bring you boys a dog for Christmas?"

"No," Harry said, giggling as he hugged her. "He's a borrowed dog, Nana."

"But we can pet him and play with him and take him for a walk whenever we want to," Bobby said.

"Why, hello, Alan," Mrs. Barrett said when she saw him. "It's so nice to see you here for this very special occasion." Audrey wished she had snapped a picture to capture the look of surprise and delight on her face.

"Thanks, Mrs. Barrett. I couldn't miss Jesus' birthday party."

Harry and Bobby opened their presents from Nana and Granddad, and of course they wanted to change into their new Roy Rogers cowboy hats and boots and fringed vests and chaps the moment they opened them. They strapped on the holsters and pistols, too.

"Now I'm a real cowboy!" Harry declared.

"Me, too!"

It was time for the birthday party to begin. Audrey slipped into the kitchen to put candles on the cake and was surprised when Mr. Barrett followed her, carrying a wrapped present. "I bought this for you, Audrey, and I just want to say . . . Well, open it first." Her fingers trembled as she pulled off the wrapping paper. She had always felt as though her father-in-law didn't quite approve of her or the decisions she made, but inside the box was a beautiful, professional stethoscope. "You're doing a fine job raising your son," he said. "I'm so proud of you. And I want to wish you all the best with your career as a nurse."

Audrey turned and hugged him tightly. "Thank you, Dad. Thank you." It was the first time she had ever called him Dad. "I'm so sorry for turning down your generous gift when you offered to pay for my nurse's training. Please forgive me for my idiotic pride in wanting to do it all myself. I would be pleased to accept your gift."

"There's nothing to forgive," he said, patting her back. "We're family. Now let me help you with those candles. There seem to be a great many of them."

Audrey laughed. "Bobby wanted to know how old Jesus was. We had to convince him that one thousand nine hundred and fifty-one candles were too many for a single cake." Mr. Barrett carried the cake to the dining room table when they finished. The adults sat down, and Audrey snapped photographs as Alan and Tom and Grandma and Grandpa Van and the Barretts opened their presents from Harry and Bobby. Each gift was met with smiles of surprise and hugs of thanks for the boys. But her greatest joy came from seeing the expressions of delight and anticipation on her son's face as he watched each person open his or her gift. Cooper liked his new ball too and growled playfully whenever someone tried to take it from him.

"They earned the money to buy these presents by doing chores," Audrey told everyone.

"And we picked them out and wrapped them all by ourselves," Bobby added.

"We're so proud of our little Wise Men," Eve said.

"Hey, everybody, come here!" Harry called. "We have to sing 'Happy Birthday' to baby Jesus." He stood beside the TV console, where the manger scene was set up, and beckoned to everyone to come over. Jesus and the other Christmas figures were still surrounded by a humorous collection of cowboys and horses and soldiers. Mr. Potato Head was there, too, and Clarabell and Flub-a-Dub from the *Howdy Doody Show*.

"Why is your candy from the country-club party

strewn all over the top?" Eve asked. She had Tom's ring on her finger and was holding his hand.

"Because everybody is bringing candy to baby Jesus for His birthday," Harry replied as if it should be obvious. The family crowded around, and Grandma Van led them in singing "Happy Birthday" to baby Jesus.

"Just look at this motley collection of misfits gathered around the manger," Eve said when they finished.

"That's the point, isn't it?" Audrey asked. "Everyone is welcome to come to Jesus."

"Even Mr. Potato Head?" Bobby said.

Audrey bent to hug him. "Yes. Even Mr. Potato Head."

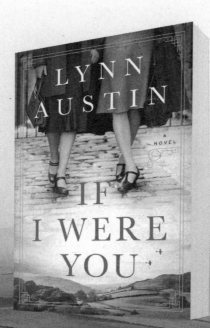

I

She lay in a lounge chair beside her mother-in-law's swimming pool, reveling in the warmth of the summer sun. The clear water reflected blue sky and cottony clouds—until four-year-old Robbie leaped into it with a shout, shattering the tranquil surface and splashing her with icy droplets. "Come in, Mommy. The water is warm!"

"Not right now, love. Maybe later." She wiped her sunglasses and opened her *Life* magazine, content to lounge in the sun's drowsy heat.

Someone called her name. "Miss Audrey?" She

swiveled to see her mother-in-law's maid hurrying from the house. "Miss Audrey? Sorry to bother you, ma'am, but you better come on inside."

"What's wrong, Nell?"

Robbie leaped into the pool again with another resounding splash, showering them both. The maid didn't seem to feel the cold spray.

"There's a woman at the door, says she's you. Even talks like you. Has a little boy and a whole pile of suitcases with her."

"What?" She scrambled up from the lounge chair, wrapping a towel around herself as if it could shield her.

"Yes, ma'am. She says she's Audrey Barrett and the little boy is the missus's grandson. Says we're expecting her."

Oh no! No, no, no! Fear tingled down her spine and raised the hair on her arms. The same stunned feeling that came seconds after a bomb detonated. She opened her mouth but nothing came out.

"Didn't know what to do," Nell said, "so I say for her and the boy to come inside and wait."

Her heart hammered against her ribs. She swallowed and finally found her voice. "I'll talk to her, Nell. Will you get Robbie out of the pool and bring him inside?"

"Yes, ma'am."

She hurried into the house barefoot, a fist of dread punching her stomach. *It can't be. Please, God . . . this can't be happening.* She halted in the hallway and peered into the foyer—and there she stood. Her best friend. Her worst fear. She held a small, dark-haired boy by the hand. She had been peeking into the home's formal living room, where Nell had been vacuuming, but turned and saw her. Her friend's eyes widened with shock. "Eve! What in the world are you doing in America?" She took a step forward as if they might embrace, then halted.

It shook Eve to hear her real name spoken again. Her heart thudded. How she wished she could shove this intruder out the door and return to a quiet afternoon beside the pool, to the life she had lived for nearly four years. Instead, she planted her hands on her hips, pretending to be brave as she had so many times before. "What are you doing here?"

"I brought my son to America to meet his father's family. . . . They live here, don't they?" She looked at the envelope in her hand as if to be sure. "This . . . this is their address . . ."

The back door slammed. A moment later, the maid came in with Robbie, still wearing his plastic floating ring, dripping water on the parquet floor. "Everything all right, ma'am?" Nell asked, looking from one to the other.

"Everything's fine." She led Nell toward the living room, speaking quietly. "We were flatmates during the war."

"Why she saying she's you?"

"I think you may have misunderstood. I'll fix my friend a glass of iced tea and then she'll be leaving."

"What about all them suitcases? You want Ollie to fetch them inside for her?"

"Never mind about the luggage. Please, continue with your vacuuming, Nell." She waited for her to go, then turned to her son. "Robbie, please take this little boy to your playroom for a few minutes."

"But I wasn't done swimming."

"We'll go back in the pool after these people leave." And they had to leave. She watched him trudge off to the first-floor playroom, battling to control her panic, then gestured for her former friend to follow her into the kitchen. The boy clung to his mother as if they were glued together. Eve fetched two glasses from the cupboard, pulled an aluminum ice cube tray from the freezer, and yanked on the lever to release the cubes.

Her damp fingers stuck to the cold metal. She remembered the day the workmen found an unexploded bomb across the street from their London flat, how it had lain there in secret for months, waiting. That was the power of secrets. Even the most carefully hidden one could explode when you least expected, demolishing the wall of lies you'd constructed around it. But she would find a way to defuse this bombshell. She wouldn't let it destroy the life she'd rebuilt, the home she had found for her son.

She poured tea into the glasses and sat down at the kitchen table, studying her friend for a moment. She was still pretty at age thirty-one with porcelain skin and amber hair, still trim and shapely. Her friend had been born with a silver spoon in her mouth, as they said, but the war had tarnished all those spoons. What mattered now was how to get rid of her. She had barely taken a sip of her iced tea or calmed her fears enough to devise a plan when Robbie slouched into the kitchen again, his baggy, wet swimsuit still dripping.

"I'm hot, Mommy. Can we go back in the pool now?"

"I'd like you to play with your new friend for a few minutes."

"He won't come with me." Eve took a good look at the boy's thick, dark hair, his coal-black eyes, and the tiny cleft in his little chin, and her heart raced faster. Anyone with two eyes would be able to see how much he resembled his father. She needed to get him and his mother out of this house before Mrs. Barrett returned. Eve pushed back her chair and stood.

"I have ice cream in my freezer at home. Would you boys like some?"

"No, I want to swim in Nana's pool!" Robbie stomped his bare foot for emphasis.

"Later. We'll swim later. After we have ice cream. Come on, let's all go to our house." Maybe if Audrey saw how happy and settled they were here in America, she would go back to England and leave them alone. "Put on your shirt, Robbie. And your shoes. Give me a minute to get dressed, too." She ducked into the powder room where her clothes hung and struggled into them, hampered by her sweaty skin.

Once dressed, she opened the front door to lead the way outside and nearly tripped over the mound of suitcases piled on the front step. "Are all of these yours?" she asked. How long was Audrey planning to stay? It looked like forever, judging by the amount of luggage.

Eve hefted two suitcases and hauled them to her car. "Let's hope everything fits in the boot. Get in the car, Robbie."

"Wait . . . why . . . ? What are you doing?" Audrey sputtered. "I'm here to visit Mr. and Mrs. Barrett."

Eve didn't reply as she shoved in the rest of the suitcases. They had to leave before Mrs. Barrett returned from her tennis match at the country club and the world Eve had created began to implode. "Just get in the car, Audrey. I'll explain later."

"But they're expecting me."

Eve squared her shoulders and willed the fear from her voice. "No. They're not expecting you. Get in the car." She held the passenger door open.

"But . . . I still don't understand what you're doing here in America. When you left Wellingford Hall, you vanished into thin air. I had no idea where you went or what became of you. And now you're here in my mother-in-law's home? You owe me an explanation, Eve."

"I saved your life, remember? You would be dead right now if it weren't for me, so please, just get in. I'll explain on the way."

Eve could see that her words had shaken Audrey.

Audrey climbed into the front seat and settled her

son on her lap. Tears slipped down her face. "We used to be friends, remember? We looked out for each other. What happened?"

"The war happened, Audrey. It changed us. And we're never going to be the same again."

Eve backed her car into the street, then sped away. They drove in silence for several minutes before Audrey spoke again. "What's going on, Eve? I want to know what you're doing here with Robert's family."

Eve's heart thudded faster. "You decided not to come to America, remember? You made up your mind to stay in England. You said Wellingford Hall was your home and you didn't want to leave it. Ever."

"Well . . . things changed. . . . But that doesn't explain why—"

"How did you get here? Boat, airplane?" Eve floored the accelerator, driving as if racing through London in her ambulance again, delivering casualties to the hospital. She barely paid attention to traffic as panic fueled her, and nearly drove past a stop sign. She slammed on the brakes so hard that Robbie tumbled onto the backseat floor. Audrey, still holding Bobby on her lap, had to brace against the dashboard. "Sorry . . . ," Eve mumbled. "You were saying . . . ?"

"We came by ship to New York City, then by train, then taxi—the same way you did, I presume. What does it matter how we—?"

"How is Wellingford Hall? I want to hear all about Mrs. Smith and Tildy and Robbins and George . . ."

"They're gone. All the servants are gone. Father sold Wellingford Hall. It's no longer our home."

Wellingford Hall—sold? Eve slowed the car. She needed a moment to absorb that bombshell. She had always imagined that she and Robbie would return for a visit one day, and it would be exactly as she remembered it. She would gather around the table in the basement with her fellow servants and talk about the past. And Mum.

Sold.

The London town house was also gone, so where would Audrey live? *Not here. Please, not here!* Eve downshifted, glancing around at the traffic, barely aware of what she was doing.

"So you decided to come to America? But surely you . . . I mean, it's very different here. Not at all like home . . ."

"The Barretts are the only family I have left. I'm moving here with Bobby."

This can't be happening.

"I wrote and told them I was coming. I don't understand why they weren't expecting me."

The letter. Eve had intercepted a letter from Audrey a month ago. She often fetched the mail for Mrs. Barrett whenever she visited because Robbie liked to chat with the postman. When she'd seen the return address, Eve had slipped the letter into her purse. She hadn't bothered to read it before tossing it into her rubbish bin at home. Now she wished she had. She could have told Audrey not to come, that the Barretts were getting on with their lives and didn't want a war bride they'd never met barging in.

Eve's panic subsided a bit as she steered her car into her neighborhood, passing rows and rows of identical bungalows. She'd thought the community looked very American when she'd first seen it, with its tidy green lawns and white picket fences. Now the neighborhood seemed stark and boring. The land had been a cow pasture before the war and the streets still looked naked with only a few spindly trees, struggling to grow. She had a fleeting image of the lush, formal gardens at Wellingford Hall, remembering the rainbow of colors, the gravel walkways, the comforting *clip-snip* of George's pruning shears.

Before the war. Before everything changed.

Audrey leaned forward to stare through the windshield as they turned in to her driveway. "This house . . . it looks like the one Robert was going to build for me."

Eve couldn't reply. She remembered the brochures and floor plans Robert had sent, remembered Audrey's anxiety and uncertainty. *"The house seems so small . . . only two bedrooms!"*

"Fewer rooms for you to clean," Eve had told her. Eve parked beneath the carport and was just opening her kitchen door for everyone when a familiar pickup truck pulled up and tooted the horn. *Tom.* He called to Eve from his open window. "Hey, Audrey!"

Eve and Audrey both turned and answered at the same time. "Yes?" Could this get any more complicated? Eve hurried to the truck, where Tom sat with his arm on the windowsill. "Hi, Tom. What brings you here?"

"I stopped by to see if you and Robbie wanted to come out to the farm with me. We're bottle-feeding a new baby lamb."

"Thanks, but we have company," she said, gesturing to them. "Maybe another time—"

"Uncle Tom! Uncle Tom!" Robbie called as he

scampered down the driveway. "Can I go out to the farm with you?"

"Not today," Eve said, catching him before he reached the truck. "We're going to have ice cream, remember?" She lifted Robbie into her arms and turned to say goodbye to Tom, but Tom wasn't looking at her. He was staring at Audrey and her son, studying them. "An old friend of mine from London stopped by for a visit," Eve said, backing away from him, inching toward the house. "We have a lot of catching up to do. Cheers, Tom! Toodle-oo!"

"Yeah, bye." He didn't move his truck. He was still staring at Bobby and Audrey.

Eve hurried back to the carport and herded everyone into the house. She pulled Popsicles from the freezer and tried to send the boys into the back garden to eat them, but Audrey's son refused to leave his mum's side. "Would you like one?" she asked Audrey. "Everyone in America eats these when it's hot outside. There's a month's worth of sugar rations in each one."

Audrey didn't seem to hear her. "Wait! Was that Tom?" she suddenly blurted. "Robert's friend, Tom? One of the Famous Four?"

Eve could have lied and said no, but the pieces of

her life were quickly slipping from her grasp like a fistful of marbles and she couldn't seem to catch them fast enough. She nodded.

"I would have loved to meet him." Audrey peered through the window in the kitchen door as if she might run down the driveway to stop him. Thankfully, Tom had driven away. "The last we heard he'd been wounded . . . somewhere in Italy, wasn't it?" Audrey asked.

"Yes. He survived, though."

"The four friends . . . ," Audrey mused. "Robert, Louis, Tom, and . . . who was the fourth?"

"Arnie."

"That's right. Robert was so distraught when he learned that Arnie had a nervous breakdown. He used to tell me stories about how the four of them grew up together and played on the same sports teams."

"Mostly basketball. It's very popular over here. Do you want one of these Popsicles?"

"How did Tom know who I was? Or . . . was he talking to you? Was he calling *you* by my name?"

"Well, I . . . He . . ."

"What's going on, Eve?" She looked puzzled, but Eve could tell the pieces were starting to fall into place. "He called you Audrey—and you answered him!"

Eve couldn't draw enough air to speak.

"You stole my place, didn't you? That's why you were at the Barretts' house!"

"Listen, Audrey—"

"You're posing as me and saying that Harry is Robert's son. You keep calling him Robbie, but his name is Harry."

"I can explain—"

"You're even living in my house—Robert's house!"

Eve stared at the floor. She didn't reply.

"How could you deceive all these people, Eve? Why would you do such a terrible thing?" Audrey looked as shell-shocked as she did after the V-1 rocket attack.

At last, Eve's fear exploded in a burst of anger. "You didn't want this life, Audrey! You were too scared and too stupid to take it after Robert died. You tossed it into the rubbish bin, so I grabbed it! This is the only home my son has ever known. I won't let you waltz in here now and steal it away from him."

"Steal it away from him? *You're* the one who has stolen *my* son's family! Bobby has a right to his grand-parents' support. He has a right to know his father's family."

"It's too late to change your mind. They're my family

272

now. This is my home, my son's home—not yours. You can't take it back." Eve didn't care how shocked or angry Audrey was. It was too late to change things now.

"But we have no other place to go!" Audrey cried.

"Neither do we!" Eve struggled to breathe as they stared at each other in silence. Their sons gazed in wide-eyed confusion at the drama taking place, the Popsicles forgotten. "Listen, Audrey. For as long as we've known each other, you've had all the advantages and I've had none. You're Audrey Clarkson—the spoiled rich girl, the aristocrat! You went to a fancy school to learn how to marry a wealthy husband, so surely you can find a man in London who'd be willing to marry Alfred Clarkson's rich little daughter. A man who could buy you a house twice as big as this one—twice as big as Wellingford Hall!"

Audrey closed her eyes as if trying to shut out Eve's words. Then she bent forward and covered her face as she began to weep. Great, heartbreaking sobs shook her slender body. Eve remembered how those cries had moved her to pity when they were children. She had crept upstairs to the forbidden part of Wellingford Hall to offer Audrey strawberries and sympathy. And friendship. But not this time. No, not this time.

A Note from the Author

EVERY NOW AND THEN, it's fun for me to write something that's completely different from my usual historical novels. *The Wish Book Christmas* was that fun extra project in an otherwise not-so-fun year. I thoroughly enjoyed revisiting best friends Eve Dawson and Audrey Clarkson and their sons, Harry and Bobby, and seeing where life had taken them after the final pages of *If I Were You*.

Inspiration sprang from my own memories of the Christmas Wish Book, published each year by Sears, Roebuck and Co. Like Bobby and Harry, my two sisters and I would study the catalogue pages, dreaming of all the presents we'd find beneath the tree on Christmas morning. Happily for me, a digital version of the original 1951 Wish Book is available online, and it was fun to walk down memory lane, remembering Tinkertoys and Lincoln Logs and Betsy Wetsy dolls.

Like Eve and Audrey, my husband and I also struggled to help our children keep the real meaning of Christmas in perspective. I let Eve and Audrey borrow some of the ideas that we came up with. We always had a birthday party and birthday cake for baby Jesus. We also made the stable and manger the focus of our celebration. Like Eve, we would read the Christmas story out loud from Scripture each year as we placed Mary and Joseph, the shepherds and Wise Men in their places. Our children are all grown, but the ritual is still part of our family's Christmas celebration.

It's my hope and prayer that *The Wish Book Christmas* will brighten and inspire your Christmas celebration this season. And that as we gaze at the humble Christ child in His manger, we'll see the greatness of Father God and remember how very much He loves us.

Have a blessed Christmas!

Lynn

Discussion Questions

1. If Eve could have one wish this Christmas, it would be a home of her own. What prevents her from believing she can accept the home Tom wants to give her? Have you ever felt you owed someone a debt you had to repay or that you didn't deserve happiness for some other reason?

2. Despite growing up in great privilege, Audrey has been living humbly since moving to America. Why is she seemingly reluctant to accept a more extravagant lifestyle for herself and her son? In what ways does her independence embolden her? How does it hold her back?

3. What are some specific things Eve and Audrey fear their sons will miss out on by not having fathers? What does God promise in Psalm 68:5 and Psalm 146:9?

4. How do Eve and Audrey determine to teach their sons the true meaning of Christmas? Do you have any traditions of sharing the joy of Christmas with others?

5. When Audrey notices that her neighbor has taken down the gold star in her window, Mrs. Herder tells Audrey about how her grief for her son Michael had become a shrine and also a punishment. What does Audrey come to understand about her own grief and the freedom love offers?

6. Tom tells Eve that she needs to start seeing herself as God sees her: "a woman who is worthy of a second chance." Think about a time you were offered a second chance. How did you feel in that moment? Have you been given opportunities to extend second or third chances to others?

7. Audrey asks Eve: "Do you think God looks at our wealth and social class to decide who's worthy of His love?" Read Matthew 7:9-11. What does Jesus say about how parents treat their children? What kinds of gifts does God the Father offer?

8. Is Santa Claus part of your family's Christmas tradition? What did you think of Audrey and Eve's attempts to combat their sons' greedy wishes? How would you handle the desires of children like Harry and Bobby?

About the Author

Lynn Austin has sold more than one and a half million copies of her books worldwide. A former teacher who now writes and speaks full-time, she has won eight Christy Awards for her historical fiction and was one of the first inductees into the Christy Award Hall of Fame. One of her novels, *Hidden Places*, was made into a Hallmark Channel Original Movie. Lynn and her husband have three grown children and make their home in western Michigan. Visit her online at lynnaustin.org.

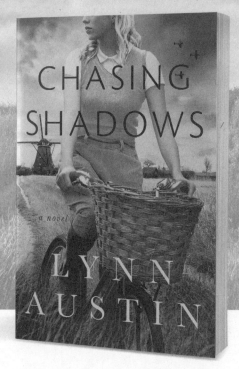